...back!

...winning stories

...Cabe's stories are dramatic, direc... ...ious. They win us with their honesty and insights. To read them is a moving and memorable experience.

Like his short novel, *Victims*, many of the stories in this book are set in the border counties of Ireland and describe the tensions and troubles of that community.

They range from childhood confrontations with the adult world to the historical intrigues of 'Victorian Fields'. They are most striking, however, when they attend to the divisions of contemporary Ireland.

In one of them, cancer becomes a metaphor for the 'Troubles'; ...other, the long title story, there ... of murders and re... isals ...mer's struggle to ... ...family's rabid ... ...ment t' at h... is

Other books by Eugene McCabe

FICTION

Victims
Royal Society of Literature (Holtby)
Award

PLAYS

King of the Castle
Irish Life Award

Pull Down a Horseman

Gale Day

HERITAGE

and other stories

by

EUGENE McCABE

THE O'BRIEN PRESS
DUBLIN

First paperback edition 1985
Published by The O'Brien Press Ltd.
20 Victoria Road Dublin 6

Originally published by
Victor Gollancz Ltd. London 1978

British Library Cataloguing in Publication Data
McCabe, Eugene
Heritage and other stories.
I. Title
823'.914[F]   PR6063.A13/

ISBN 0-86278-079-9

10   9   8   7   6   5   4   3   2   1

Origination: Redsetter Ltd.

Printed by: O'Brien Promotions Ltd.

ACKNOWLEDGEMENTS
"Truth" was published in *Aquarius*; "Roma" was
published in *Threshold*; "Music at Annahullion"
was published in *The Irish Press*. "Cancer" was
published in *The Dublin Magazine*, it received
the Writer's Award: Prague International, 1974.

CONTENTS

For my mother
who sees things
otherwise
this book is
dedicated with love

TRUTH

HE COULD SEE through the glass door of the livingroom. The brass hood was bright over the coal fire. Bridie bent down in the hall, her mouth to his ear, and whispered:

"The minute your mother says, come back out to the kitchen." His father and the two priests were drinking out of the special glasses and smiling. One was small and grey and the other heavy, red and fat. He had to shake hands with both as his mother said their names.

"A dead ringer for you, Eddie," one said.

The other said: "Yes, a replica. . . ."

Then the questions: "Is this the youngest? What age? . . . What class, who is your teacher? Do you like school?" and they always let on to be shocked when he said "No" and they would ask "Why?", but when they asked: "Which do you like best, Scotland or Ireland?" that was a trap, so he said now "I don't know."

"You don't know?" the big priest asked. "No flies on that boy!"

"Not from the dew of the grass he gets that," the small priest said.

His father laughed: "You'd think butter wouldn't melt in his mouth, but he's a rogue you know, a trickster, you wouldn't have a notion what goes on in his head."

Frank could feel himself blushing. Sometimes things did go on in his head that he'd never say to anyone, and he did have a secret with Bridie. His father was joking about being a trickster, it was a thing to say for the visitors, like the priest saying about no flies. It was the way grown up people talked to children, they didn't really mean what they said. Once Bridie said: "I could eat you", but she only meant she could give him a kiss and a hug. Sometimes her sister Maggie came at night, when his mother and father were out.

Maggie brought lemonade and chocolate biscuits, and sometimes toffee apples—that was a secret. She didn't live in Rutherglen, she lived in the middle of Glasgow. She wasn't well; you could tell from her face. His mother had a softer voice than either Bridie or Maggie and could play the piano for a long time without stopping. Everyone clapped and said: "That's beautiful, Angela", and asked her to play again. Then they would all look at the ceiling and listen. When his mother played the piano his father kept tapping with his fingers on the side of the chair. He liked people to sing and recite. He sang "The Pale Moon was Rising above the Green Mountains". Tonight there would be no singing or piano, they were going out to Paisley somewhere, where his Uncle Petey kept a ham and egg shop. Uncle Petey said everyone who worked in the shop stole things from him, he said you couldn't trust anyone any more—take the garters off the virgin. Once a month Uncle Petey had to have a man nurse in the house, or he would break all the furniture and all the windows, and Frank often heard his father say it was because he married such a stupid woman; that was Aunt Molly. She wrote stories for Holy magazines. You could buy them in the church at Rutherglen. Every story had a miracle. His father was pouring more whiskey into all the glasses, and one of the priests was trying to stop him. His father said: "We're going to a dry house." Then his mother called him over and said:

"Out to Bridie now, love, and then bed."

"Are you going to cards?"

"Yes, say goodbye to Father Moore and Father Duffy."
He said what he was told to say always:

"Good night everybody."

And they all said together, "Good night Frank."

"A dead ringer," he heard the big priest say.

Bridie must have known his parents were going out.
She was sitting at the kitchen table eating her tea. It was
near dark outside. He could see the concrete yard from
the street lights and across the road the high wall that
went around Dr. Slowey's place, and the high railings
round Queen's Park. There were fields round Dr. Slowey's,
and cows. An old man called Ferguson came to milk the
cows night and morning.

Every day in the year Bridie took him for a walk in the
park. There were owls and squirrels there, and a rockery,
and some of the stones in the rockery were faces. In a
hollow there was a bandstand like a stage, and a round
iron tent and you could sit there in the summer and
listen to music. The men wore costumes. There was a
place for playing too, swings, see-saws, and skip-arounds,
and in the middle of the park, a fat lady sat on a chair
under a sort of small bandstand, "The old Queen" Bridie
said, "she's dead now." Once he heard his father say,
"If the Sloweys had their way they'd sooner kneel to
that fat old bitch than go to Mass."

Dr. Slowey's wife wore very big hats, and the Slowey
boys were a good bit older. They went to school in
England. They talked a different way. There was a tall
flag-pole near Slowey's house. It was higher than the
trees round the house. On special days they put up a

flag, and they were the days his father got angry. "Irish
my arse," he would say, and his mother said, "Hush,
Eddie." She didn't like words like arse. Frank had been
in Slowey's surgery twice. It was old, faded and dark,
just as everything in their own house was new, shiny
and bright. He asked his mother why.

"Truth is they have no money, love."

"No money?"

"Not *real* money."

It was hard to understand why his father got angry,
and even though his mother didn't use words like his
father, he could tell she didn't like the Sloweys either,
even though he was the family doctor. What was hard
to understand was how people without money could
have a cow and a man to milk it, and a man in the
garden, and a special man to drive the car, even though
it was the oldest car in Glasgow. The car had no roof.
"All show," his father said, "their auld fella was a
drunken tailor from Tyrone and a bad one at that." It
was hard to know the truth about a lot of things.

"Sit down, love," Bridie said.

She put a plate of beans on the table. His mother came
in and told Bridie she would be late and left a telephone
number. Every time she was going out she stood in the
middle of the kitchen under the electric light in her
furry coat with a basket of mending showing Bridie the
different things to mend, and talking about 'phone calls,
and fireguards and keeping the chain on the door, and
how there was a murder every week in Glasgow, and
sometimes two or three. She said the same things to
Bridie every time and Bridie said: "Yes Mam . . . I know
Mam . . . I will Mam. I'll phone if there's anything . . .

goodbye Mam." There never was anything; nothing ever happened. It meant he could stay up late, and watch Bridie sewing or look at comics. Then his mother was kissing him, then she was gone.

Through the kitchen window Bridie watched the car reversing out of the garage. It turned right and went out by Cathkin. Then he was standing on a chair in the scullery helping her to dry dishes. Even so she was still a good bit bigger. The 'phone rang and she went out and talked a long time to her sister Maggie. When she came back to the sink she stood looking a long time and thinking.

"Would you like a wee journey, Frank?"

"Where?"

"To see Maggie."

"In a tram?"

"If you want."

"Would it be dark?"

"It's dark now."

"Is it a long way to Maggie?"

"About half an hour."

"That's a long way."

"Get your coat, hurry."

Walking down Mill Street to Rutherglen Bridie asked:

"Can you keep a secret, Frank?"

"You know I can."

"No matter what?"

"I wouldn't tell on you, Bridie."

"I don't think you would, well this is a secret."

"What is?"

"Going to see Maggie."

"Why?"

"It just is, very secret."

"Why, Bridie?"

She didn't answer so he asked again.

"Because you should be in your bed, and I should be mending. If your mother found out she'd ate the face off me."

That was true all right. Once his mother came back early with a headache and was very cross with Bridie because he was still up. He was very sorry for Bridie that night, it was really his fault.

The tram was full downstairs. They went upstairs. He sat on Bridie's lap to make room for a lady. Cars, coloured lights, traffic lights, lorries, taxis, big advertisements outside picture houses, the noise of engines and horns humming and booming, mixed with the sound of rain, and water running down the glass of the tram window, and the tram full of smoke and people coughing. They got off near the river. They walked along for a while. He could not see over the wall to the river.

"Is it far where we're going, Bridie?"

"A brave wee bit, are you tired?"

"No."

They went down dark streets. The rain had stopped. The pavements were wet. They passed close after close, some lit, some black. In the black ones he could make out white faces, sometimes a woman's, sometimes boys'. From a close a boy shouted something, a very bad word. Bridie didn't look back or say anything.

"Why did they shout that, Bridie?"

"They know no better, pass no remarks."

The close they turned into had no light on the staircase. He held Bridie's hand as they went up, his other

hand against the tiled wall. It was wet. There were a lot
of tiles cracked or missing. There was an odd smell like
the dark pit under the garage. They went up a lot of
stairs. Then they came to a door and Bridie knocked. A
man opened it. He had fuzzy reddish hair and glasses.
He was wearing braces over his shirt. He had no collar.
Sometimes his father shaved like that. The man with the
glasses hadn't shaved for two days or maybe three. When
he saw it was Bridie, he didn't say "hello", or kiss or
shake hands, he just said:

"She's not here."

They were standing in a narrow hall. There was
nothing in the hall. Bridie walked past the man and
went through the door. From the room she called:

"Come on, Frank."

He passed the man and went into a square room.
There was a black range, a sink full of washing, and
beside it clothes drying on a rack, a double bed in the
corner, and dirty dishes everyway on a draining board.
There were two children asleep on a mattress in another
corner. There was a table with a shiny cloth and four
chairs round the table. One of the chairs had no back.
The smell in the room was worse than the smell in the
hall, like when a person got sick, but different. There
was one window, and no other door out of the room.

"Where is she?" Bridie asked.

"Out."

For a while they looked at each other and said
nothing. The man was blinking behind his glasses. Bridie
said:

"Sit there at the table, love, and look at your comic."

He went to the table and opened his comic. He tried

to look at the funny pictures. Bridie was talking in a low voice, almost a whisper. He couldn't hear anything, she seemed upset. The man wasn't bothered. He stood and looked at her. Then he was startled to hear Bridie say:

"Your fault, you lazy, drunken blackguard. Your fault, not hers."

The man said:

"Shut your mouth or I'll break your back."

That was a terrible thing to say. If you broke a person's back they would never walk again. Frank looked up at the man's face. He did not look angry.

"She's my sister."

"She's a born bitch, she'd do it for nothing."

"Liar, you make her," Bridie was screaming. She came to the table and put her hands on it. Frank kept looking at his comic, but he could feel the table with Bridie's hands on it like when you touched the fridge, a kind of shiver. Then the outside door opened.

"That's her now," the man said.

And Maggie came in. She looked awful tired. When she saw Bridie she began to cry. Then they were all talking in very loud voices, and he couldn't understand what happened, but the man was pulling at Maggie's handbag, and Maggie wouldn't let it go. When the man got it he emptied it upsidedown on the table. Bits of things came out, coins and lipstick rolled over his comic and off the table. Then the man was pulling at Maggie's clothes, it was terrible. He pulled off her coat, and put his hands in the pockets, then he pulled at her dress. When the dress tore, she had nothing on under the dress and she was screaming. Then Bridie was screaming and trying to stop him. The man pushed Bridie away with his elbow, and knocked down Maggie. Then he was kicking Maggie on her stomach, and between her legs, and the children on the mattress were screaming, and Frank was so frightened he couldn't move. Then he saw Bridie on the floor, with her arms round the man's legs to stop him from kicking Maggie. That made the man begin to fall. For a moment he knew the man would fall towards him. He tried to get off the chair; something hit the side of his head.

Back now in bed in his own room, his father and Dr. Slowey were staring out the window, looking towards Queen's Park and Cathkin. They were talking in low voices. His face was swollen out. His mother sat on his bed. She asked again:

"How did it happen, Frank?"

"I don't know."

"Why don't you know?"

"I forget."

Dr. Slowey looked over from the window, he had a white face like the statue of the Sacred Heart on the landing, but no beard. He said:

"You must tell your mother how it happened." Frank thought for a moment and said:

"What does Bridie say?"

There was a long silence, and then Dr. Slowey said:

"Bridie says she doesn't know how you got such a bump."

"I fell downstairs."

"When?"

"Last night."

"How?"

"I was going for a drink of water and I fell." There

was another very long silence. Up to this they had only asked questions, now his mother said:

"You are not telling the truth, Frank."

She nodded towards his father. His father left the room and came back with Bridie. Her face looked very odd, you'd know she'd been crying a lot.

"Frank says he fell downstairs, Bridie."

"True as God, Mam, I don't know what happened to the child."

Again there was a silence. Bridie had told a lie; he too to save her, he would have to stick to it no matter what. She often told small lies, but this was a very big one. His mother said:

"Frank, we know you're lying, dear, why can't you tell us?"

"It's the truth, Mama."

"You're telling lies, you were seen, both of you, going down Mill Street after we left last night, and you were seen again at the tram stop in Rutherglen."

He looked from face to face. They knew that; that was true. Bridie seemed lost and frightened. He said:

"I didn't tell, Bridie, I didn't say anything." Then Bridie began to cry. It was awful because none of the others said anything, so Frank said:

"It wasn't Bridie's fault, she was just trying to stop the man kicking Maggie on the floor."

That seemed to make things worse. Bridie left and then they all went out and he was alone. It was coming on dark again. His mother brought up tea and he had to tell about the tram, the walk along the river, the dark streets, the man and Maggie, the children and the mattress. Some parts he left out, like the words the boy

shouted. He had to say about the fight. He knew from
the way his mother nodded that she believed him. He
was almost asleep when Bridie came in and told him
she was going back to Ireland.

"Why, Bridie?"

"I have to."

"I didn't tell."

"I know, love—not your fault."

Frank said: "It's the bad man's fault, the kicking man."

"He's not bad, he drinks too much, that's all—like your
Uncle Petey."

Her voice sounded odd.

"I must go, love."

She gave him a kiss and went out of the room. For a
long time that night he tried to understand what the
truth was. Was it true what she said, that the kicking
man was not bad? It was terrible what he was doing,
but then his Uncle Petey smashed every window in his
own house, but that was just silly, not the same as
kicking a woman on the floor. If that wasn't bad, then
what was? Did Bridie just say he wasn't bad because he
was Maggie's husband, a kind of brother. Why did she
not tell the truth? His father could visit his brother
Petey, why could Bridie not visit her sister Maggie.
Why was it secret? And when Maggie came at night,
why did that have to be secret? And why was Bridie
going now so sudden? He couldn't understand any of it.

Next morning Bridie was gone. He asked his mother
and was told "She got the Belfast boat". He felt suddenly
very unhappy. She had said last night she was going back
to Ireland, but he knew now he would never see her
again. Where was she now? In Belfast somewhere, or

getting a bus back to Strabane. Maybe he would write to her. That evening his father came in and talked a while. He asked his father about Bridie.

"Sad business," he said.

"Did she have to go?"

"Yes."

His father refused to talk any more about it. When he was almost asleep he heard his mother saying:

"I wouldn't mind the headscarves or the cutlery or the bits and pieces from the fridge, the rashers and God knows what, but taking a child that age into the middle of the Gorbals. . . ."

There was a silence.

"If they take anything, they'll take everything. Dr. Slowey's right, they're all the same: they lie as they breathe. Truth is you can't trust them, any of them."

VICTORIAN FIELDS

PETTY SESSIONS (IRELAND)
ACT 1851 14 & 15 Vict. Cap. 93
FORM A.a: INFORMATION

May 10th: 1872

STATEMENT BY ALICE DUFFY WHO SAITH ON HER OATH:
I remember yesterday morning the 9th day of the present
month. I was in my house at Drumbane about ten o'clock
in the morning. I'd come in from milking the four cows.
My husband James Duffy was in the bed. His brother
Oweny lives with us now close on a year. He was putting
herrings on the pan. The half of them was scattered on
the fire. He is seprate this past three years from his
wife Lizzie who lives in the town-land of Arasala. He
told me once she was a mad whore like most women.
Like all the Duffys he is a bit touched himself. This
brother Oweny has a great spite on me. It's my belief he
made my husband more bitter than he was. I know the
reason. One night when he was a short time here he
came back from Ballybay with drink taken. My husband
was playing cards at a neighbours house. Up to this time
I was very civil with Oweny. I asked him that night
would he like a bite to eat. "I know what I'd like" he
said "and I know what you'd like." He was fornenct
me at the fire and exposed himself. "Don't do a thing
like that Oweny" I said, "It's a mistake, you've too much
taken." "Damn the mistake" he said "Did you ever see

the like of that." "Shame on you Oweny" I said "I'm your brother's wife." "And your child's not his" he said "and well you know it." I said if he didn't make himself decent I'd go straight for Sergeant Riley. I know well that he's a coward. He talks loud and has a name for showing himself to women and is the laugh of the country. I told him to have more wit. I wasn't afraid of him or any man. He got up then and tried to assault me indecently. I pushed him away.

From that night he behaves bitter towards me and my husband is worse in his manner. He wouldn't believe my story. He told me that I had tempted his brother Oweny. I asked him how. No decent man he said would talk of what I'd done. On my oath this is lies. My husband has a grudge on account of the land. He brought £60 the day we married. The land and the four cows is mine. At the start he tried to get the land in his own name. I put him off. He took this bad and nothing I done after was any good in his eyes. Five years back when we first married he abused me so much I went to the priest in Ballybay Fr. Alex McMahon. The Priest's housekeeper Bridget Hanley closed the door in my face and said the likes of me should not be let next or near a priest. She left me standing in the street. I know now for sure my husband turned the priest against me because when the priest came out to talk to me he wouldn't let me tell my story but let a shout at me and said I was a disgrace and a scandal to the whole country and the Catholic faith and that only a saint could put up with me. I said "God help me father what have I done." "What have you not done woman," he shouted, "the devil's work."

My husband took the notion that the child I was

carrying was not his. On account of this he abused me day in, day out, and started into drink, telling the clergy and the whole country a dose of lies about me and my brother Michael. He's still bitter about the land.

Yesterday morning when I came in from milking, I saw the herrings scattered in the fire, I got fire tongs to take out the herrings.

"Don't mind them," Oweny said.

"I'm only giving you a hand," I said.

"I don't want your hand," he said and pushed me away from the fire. I told him not to do that again or I'd break a crock across his skull. He then let a roar and told me to get to hell out of the house while he was at his breakfast. I told him to talk quiet and think again. I told him it was my house and my food. He was living on my charity and if he was any kind of man it was himself would get out of my house and go back to his own woman Lizzie and show her the scenery he showed me one night at the fire. I know it was a mistake to say that, but I couldn't stop myself. He then struck me on the mouth with a fish. I cried and said "Don't do that with the herrings I bought dear for my own child" and he shouted "To hell with you and your bastard you whore you" and he caught hold of me and pushed me out the door and gave me a kick with the toe of his boot. The pain of that went up through me and I fell holding my stomach. He then gave me a box of his clenched fist in my left eye when I was kneeling. I screamed at him that I was carrying a child. "It's no Duffy," he shouted. "Take care or I'll kick you and it in a bog-hole."

In all this commotion my husband was upstairs in bed. I don't know if he heard. To my knowledge he never

got up before mid-day. Most days it's nearer one
o'clock.

After I was abused by Oweny I went up to a neighbours house Pat Ward. His sister Mary bathed my face
and told me to go and see Sergeant Riley at Ballybay
and make a complaint.

SIGNED: ALICE DUFFY

PETTY SESSIONS (IRELAND)

ACT 1851 14 & 15 Vict. Cap. 93

FORM A.a.: INFORMATION

To-day at Hollands Forge I Cautioned Owen Duffy of
Drumbane and late of Arasala. When I served A Sum-
mons he shouted abuse about his sister-in-law and asked
me to take the following Information.

SIGNED: SGT. HUGH REILLY

STATEMENT BY OWEN DUFFY WHO SAITH ON HIS OATH:
When I first came to my brother's house about a year
ago I noticed my sister-in-law Alice Duffy strange in her
mind. She would shout that all about the place would
be taken from her. One day she had stones in her hand
to throw at whoever came. One day she asked me to
look about the house and yard for her brother Michael
McKenna and herself began to look, talking and crying.
Her brother Michael is in America this six years. Some-

times she is troubled beyond what a man can understand. Nobody she says can do any work right about the place only herself, and she is all the time complaining about the work she has to do. I have my own opinion of that work. She's a great one for travelling through the country looking for a stray calf or a lost hen and this takes her to strange townlands and men. I believe myself she is a woman of low character.

My brother James has great patience. This last while she has been trying to run away. Yesterday she flung a scald of spud water at the two of us and said she would drown herself and her child in a bog-hole. She buys herrings and the like and forgets about them 'till they smell the house. The day before yesterday when I went to cook a herring she went out of her mind. I believe my sister-in-law Alice Duffy is a dangerous lunatic and I pray she may be committed to Monaghan asylum.

May 12th:

ADDITIONAL INFORMATION OF ALICE DUFFY WHO SAITH ON HER OATH:

When my husband James Duffy found out I went to Sgt. Riley he began to call me a "whore out of hell" a "bitch to end all bitches" I said nothing. I am well used to that class of talk so he come up close to me and said ... "You're a cunt woman nothing more or less than a cunt" I scratched his face and pulled out a go of his whiskers. He then pushed me away and took a plough reins from the dresser. He thrashed me about the kitchen with the reins until I was not fit to scream. When my child Andy tried to stop him he cuffed him and knocked him down. Every time he cut me with the reins he said, "Where's Sgt. Riley now?" Then he put my child out of the house and told me I'd get the rope proper. He said he would hang me. I was afraid and took the child and slept in Pat Wards kitchen. My back and stomach still have the marks of the reins. I showed them to Dr. MacAllister. I am in fear and dread of my husband and my brother-in-law and will not go next or near the house until they have been charged and locked away.

May 13th:

INFORMATION OF JAMES DUFFY WHO SAITH ON HIS OATH:
I believe my wife Alice Duffy has been deranged in her mind since I married her six years ago. The truth is I married a bad one. She's an unnatural woman. She was two months gone with child when we married. I asked her to name the father. She would not say. I spoke strong. I stayed at her night and day till I got it from her. She screeched at me that the father was her brother Michael from Lisaduff. When I heard this from her own mouth it sickened my stomach. I walked to her brothers farm four miles. I faced him in his own yard:

"Your sister says you made a whore out of her and that the cub is yours."

"She's sick then," he said.

"Is she a liar," I asked him.

"No man would do the like with his sister." So I asked him who it was and he said, "No woman could be watched." A month after I spoke to him he sold his land and left for America.

That same day I went back to Drumbane. My wife

was in the haggard behind the house milking. I went up to her and told her what her brother had said. She began to shiver and cry. I told her to quit whining, and tell the truth. After a while she said there was no woman in the whole country as unhappy as herself. So I said, "What about me?" As God's my judge she stared up at me her face all twisted and said, "I don't give a snotter for you or any Duffy. I never did nor I never will. There's only one man I care about." I said he didn't care much about her. She screamed, "I was ignorant and knew nothing." I said I understood well that she was an un-natural woman. From that day out I hardly spoke to her. I worked anywhere but Drumbane.

This last while she is a brave bit worse and talks a lot to herself. She will not talk to me or my brother but she told a neighbour Mary Ward that when she tries to pray her head is full of cursing and black notions and death.

Three days ago she screamed and shouted for twenty minutes that a devil was in the house and after that she threw boiling water at my brother and myself. Later in the day she took a turn and said she would be a stiff corpse before long and that something terrible would happen. I sent my brother Oweny for Canon Hackett. She told the Canon in front of us that we would not let her out of the house. That we kicked her and cuffed her and that she was worked to death, that both of us hated herself and her child and that we wanted her locked up to get our hands on the bit of land. She said we would starve her child to death. The Canon then took her down to the low room and she quieted a little. Later at black dark she got out a window with the child and made off across the fields. I followed her with

Oweny for fear she would do harm to herself. She stayed that night at Wards house and has been there since. I know she has made statements to the Constabulary. I would say they are a string of lies. I don't know what she said about my brother and myself but the whole country knows the truth about herself and her brother Michael. I believe my wife Alice is now a dangerous lunatic. I pray she may be arrested and committed to Monaghan asylum.

I swear this statement is true.

SIGNED: JAMES DUFFY

ROMA

MARIA CAME OUT of the kitchen with a fish supper. "It's here, Mickey, on the counter."

Wiping the mock terrazzo he thanked her from his knees, no press stud in his cap, the peak almost level with his foggy glasses. He seemed blind. She sat at a formica-topped table near the juke-box, opened a magazine and watched him get up. Not his fault the way he looked, yellow teeth in red gums, the face white like a monk's. That was why kids chucked things as he pulled his barrow through streets, women giggling in doorways when their men tonguefarted or used the Holy Name. A bit of crack, they thought, to see him drop the handcart and bless himself. Of course he was odd, out praying like that from house to house, and when he wasn't carting brock or clearing dumps he sat in the loft he shared with Joe the Bush down their yard. Joe was part-time beggar, full-time drunk. One day she asked Joe what Mickey did in the loft.

"Never done cuttin' slips from wee Holy Books and stickin' them in copy books with Holy pictures . . . the kind of thing an auld nun puts in her time at." Holy Mickey, mad Mickey, Mickey the mutter, Mickey the Brock, Mickey Longford, he had nicknames enough to do ten townlands. She had never really bothered much with him till yesterday when Connolly took him away to load pigs. He had left the garden in a hurry, his jacket bunched in the fork of a tree. Hanging clothes on the line she could see a wad of stuff in the breast pocket.

There was no one about. Under an apple tree she went through the wad, bits of paper, clippings, mostly hand-printed with different coloured biros.

She read:

> c/o Digacimo
> Cafe Roma
> The Diamond
> The World is Dying
> The Town is Dying.

A Cure for the World

Shut the Pubs
Shut the Dance Halls
Shut the Picture Houses
Put cars off the roads
More Penance
Live Modest
Think on death day and night,
Bad thoughts make bad Talk
Makes man do bad things
After that the head goes
Burn Dirty Books, Papers and Pictures
Pray for my father in the mental, keep him
from Hell
Pray for my Mother in her grave at Knockatallon
Pray for Annie and Josie who have forgot me
Pray for Joe the Bush who sins every night
Pray for people who shout at me and childer who
mock me
Pray for Mr. and Mrs. Digacimo, and M
Above all things keep M pure

Cellotaped to a piece of cardboard was a picture of the
Virgin waistdeep in cotton wool. Printed carefully underneath:

MARIA

May God scatter over her path the Flower of His
Divine Benediction

She began to feel she had encroached and fumbled the
wad. Medals, scapulars, notes and letters fell on the grass.
As she gathered them one caught her eye. It began with
her name:

Maria I must tell you things The truth In the yard
at night I often stand under your room I would like
to be the light in your room I could see you then and
give light for your homework I would stay awake
all night watching you breathe that's all Odd times
too I would like to be slippers you wear about the
house and cafe or the sheets in your bed or your comb
in the streets I am crying to myself because of you
my life is terrible and there is nothing I can do the
squeal of pigs I hate and the smell of them makes me
sick every day I see little pigs sucking out of big ones
and the big ones breed like rats acres of them out at
clonfad a town of pigs beside the town when they
are fat for the factory I help load them on the lorries
the smell is awful on a hot day blood and squeeling in
the factory yard do they know I often wonder
most people eat sausages even you I don't it makes
me sick everything does in this world except you I

B

can't explain it nothing is new to me before I sleep
you are my gate to heaven when I wake you are my
morning star and the truth is the heart is broke inside
me because of how I feel and I can never tell you or
give you this letter I write this because it is the
truth maybe I'll give it to you sometime but I don't
think so

Guilty, she had gathered the stuff and put it back in the
wad. All that evening she felt disturbed. It broke her
sleep and this morning she woke early. All day it had
been with her and now near the juke-box she waited,
watching him begin to eat.

He could feel her eyes. Sometimes of a Saturday when
the cafe was closed she came in like this and sat looking
through a magazine, an overall over her school uniform.
Odd times she'd play a record on the machine or move
about by herself, making noises with her fingers. Other
times she'd join her mother and father in the kitchen.
They sat there most Saturday nights when the place was
shut, reading out of foreign papers, hard workers who
kept to themselves. No friends; much like myself.

"How old are you, Mickey?"

She was looking at him very straight, eyes in her head
like no other girl or woman body he ever knew.

"Is that a cheeky thing to ask?"

"I'm six and thirty."

She went back to her magazine. He looked up at the
panel above the steel chipper, painted in shopgloss by
Murray the decorator; Pope John smiling before Saint
Peter's, hand upraised in blessing; beside him President
Kennedy smiling before the White House, hands in jacket

pocket addressing the world through a megaphone. He put a chip in his mouth.

"Why are you so grey?"

"The breed of me, nature I suppose."

"Are you long left home?"

"I quit home when my mother died. I was glad to quit."

"But you're from this country?"

"I'm a Longford man, here this brave while. I mind when you were born, people sayin' 'them Italians have a daughter'."

"You were here then, Mickey?"

"About the town."

"Working?"

"When I could."

"At what?"

"Anything."

"And your people; what did they do?"

"The auld fellow was a blacksmith when he was sober . . . he drank wild."

"Is he dead too?"

"In the Mental, below in Mullingar: God blacked his mind, he broke my mother's heart, let the roof fall in, and the whole place go to rack. I couldn't stop him. I've two sisters married in England."

"You see them?"

"No."

"Do they write?"

"No."

"Don't you?"

"Not this brave while."

"They have fambleys of their own, it's natural."

He couldn't keep looking in her eyes so he looked away. She put money in the machine and played a record. It made a noise like pigs being castrated to the sound of drums; when it stopped she asked:

"Do you ever see him, your father?"

"He didn't know me last time, and let a shout: 'I have no son, I'm the Holy Ghost, I have no son.' Then he started in to laugh and giggle and wink and said all classes of bad things. It's on account of his rotten life. God's punishment for the dark things he had done when he was drunk."

"What things? Was he bad?"

"I'd call him bad."

"What did he do?"

"He was bad."

"Papa says you shouldn't be sleeping down the yard with Joe or carting brock about the streets. He says it's a great pity of you, that you're a strange person."

"Every man has some oddness."

She had never talked close before. He felt clumsy. He moved his knife about the table.

"Am I annoying you?"

"No."

"If I didn't ask you'd say nothing. Sometimes you go a month without saying a word. Why?"

"No call to ... anyway ..."

"Yes?"

"You're too young."

"For what?"

"To know."

"What?"

"Maria! Maria!" Mrs. Digacimo's voice called high in the house.

"Si, Mama?"

The voice said something in their speech. As she got up to leave she said:

"You'll have to tell me what I don't know. I'll be back."

He watched her walk up the terrazzo floor under the fluorescent lighting past Pope John and President Kennedy, past the glossy murals of old buildings and bridges falling down across fields, past the tower going sideways and streets full of boats, and through the beaded string opening that led to the house.

What was it he couldn't tell her? There were things a grown man couldn't tell a growing girl, specially her. He couldn't say the loft he shared with Joe the Bush faced a pub entry and how night about he could hear the pissing and puking, the gropes and groans of men and women, or of how he saw his auld fellow drunk once in a shed, or remark on how Joe the Bush abused himself night after night. Even to-night when he came in to wash the floor Cissy Caffery and young Mulligan sat on facing each other. Mulligan had his hand up Cissy's skirt and she not fifteen and the two of them talking and laughing with no trace of shame. Course they were young. You had to allow for that. Maybe God would look gentle on hot blood, but there were other things so bad you couldn't scour them from your mind. The world was sick and the more he saw the worse it got. Sometimes it seemed God was deaf or blind or gone asleep. Sometimes it seemed there was no cure.

The lights in the cafe went out and the hood of the

chipper caught the street lighting, and made the two
Johns a pair of grinning ghosts. He heard someone again
on the staircase.

Maria came into the cafe and made her way through
the dark tables to where she had left her magazine. Still
there; alone. The street lights made him seem unreal, like
the morning early she looked down from her window to
the yard. He was standing against the gable of the
coach house, grey face and head, arms outstretched. She
had put on her dressing-gown and watched. Holy Mickey,
Mickey the mutter, Mickey Longford. What she had read
in the wallet was so strange, somehow private, she
meant to keep to herself, but to-day when Ursula Brogan
began boasting again about that old Ward man who
always stopped her and held her hand she found herself
talking about Mickey. Ursula listened and said :

"Ah God, that's awful, I'd straighten him out, Maria,
honest to God I would."

"It's nice someway."

"The Blessed Virgin . . . It's pukey!"

"But I am a virgin."

"Not the Blessed Virgin. It's not right I'd tell him if I
were you."

"Tell him what?"

He moved in the chair as she approached. She could
just make him out.

"Did we leave you in the dark again, Mickey?"

"No odds, I'm for bed."

She moved to see him better and said :

"What am I too young to know?"

Mickey heard her voice but didn't know what she had
asked. It was darkness all round but where she stood it

seemed light. For a moment he thought he'd like to go down on his knees and kiss her hands and feet.

"Pardon, Miss."

"What am I too young to know?"

"The world is bad, Miss."

"Sure I know that."

"And this town is rotten like the bad end of a city."

"Ah come off it, Mickey, how do you know?"

"I hear it and see it."

"Where?"

"Down the yard, round the town, out the country, everywhere. No one thinks of God or dying or what comes after."

She looked out towards the street. She was holding the magazine against her breast, exactly as the Virgin held the child in a picture he had, but much younger, more beautiful. He wanted to say he'd die to keep her the way she was, clear of the Mulligans and Joe the Bush, the pubs, the drunks, the women in the doorways, the pigs and the dance-halls, the brock, all the ugliness of life. She was like a sloping field one spring day he remembered long ago in Longford, high high hedges that hid houses, roads, lanes. You could see nothing but sky. Just grass, thorn blossom and the sky. It was so beautiful he felt that it would blind him. He wanted to sleep and never wake. That was what she was like looking out in the street. He had the same feeling now that he got in the field, but how did you say a thing like that? Then he heard himself say:

"You're like a field."

"A field?"

Did she give a little giggle? He wasn't sure.

"At home near Knockatallon. It had high hedges."

He knew he couldn't say the thing he thought.

"A field in May ... thorn ditches ... there was a power of blossom."

For quite a time neither said anything. Then Maria said:

"I'm not like that; I know what you mean but I'm not like that. When you said a field I nearly laughed because I was in a field last week with Ursula Brogan behind the football pitch. We followed Cissy Caffery there and two boys from the secondary. She's a wagon. She did it with them one after the other, and we watched."

The street lights went out. The silence was odd. She felt she must go on talking:

"I wouldn't do that but if I loved a fellow I'd lie with him and make him happy. That's the truth about me. Are you there, Mickey?"

"Yes."

"You heard what I said?"

"Why did you say it?"

"It's true."

"You shouldn't."

"Have watched or told you?"

He didn't answer. His chair scraped and she saw him move towards the kitchen.

"Mickey!"

He went through the kitchen out the back door down the yard. She could feel heat in her face and an odd beat in her heart. It had seemed right to tell him, but as she spoke it sounded blunt, ugly and final as though she were deliberately destroying something; false too because she'd been disgusted and didn't say so. "But I didn't mean any-

thing" she thought. What made her say it when she
knew what he'd written and how he thought about her,
it was like mocking a cripple or putting poison in a baby's
bottle.

She went down the yard and looked up at the loft; no
light. Even if she did see him how could she unsay what
she had said. She felt now she was worse than Cissy
Caffery, that she had done something very stupid and
very wrong and there was no way she could undo it.

"I'm sorry, Mickey. Honestly I'm sorry."

He sat in the loft on the iron frame bed. Twice Joe the
Bush said something to him. Mickey heard words but
couldn't give them meaning.

"Are you deaf, man?"

"What?"

"Why don't you spake?"

"What?"

"Arra God!"

Mickey lay back on the bed dressed and looked
through the skylight at the stars. Joe the Bush began to
shift about, abusing himself as he did most nights. The
springs skreeked and the broken castor scraped on the
wormy boards. Mickey listened.

"God sees you, Joe."

"For Christ's sake shut up, you eejit. They'll lock you
up like your father."

Then Joe was snoring and Mickey was counting hours
from the Church. Again and again he scoured his mind
with prayer, but he could see her eyes seeing what she
said she'd seen, her mouth telling nakedness and sin and
for an instant he saw her lying with Joe the Bush and he

B*

woke startled and sweating. Why had she said such
things? Would she earn Hell too with filthy hags, a
hag herself, her mouth black and screaming, damned?
What was happening to the world? Men, women and
children walking to damnation. The stars were mostly
gone when he found himself saying: "House of Gold,
Arch of the Covenant, Gate of Heaven, Morning Star,
Morning Star, Morning Star." Winter and there were
stars over the frosted field and he was kneeling on hard
ground waiting for the Mother of God, Christ born
again in this field at Knockatallon. He'd be there and
the world saved. An ass carrying a small cloaked figure
came through the frozen gap. A hatted man behind kept
prodding. He could see it all very clearly, even the
mincing trot of the ass, its tail wagging ... It was Saint
Joseph and the Virgin Mary. The ass came up the field
to where he was kneeling. Mary dismounted and began
opening a pack. He could tell she was very young, a
girl. Saint Joseph made an arch of blackened ash rods
and pulled a tat of bags across it. He lit a fire at the
opening of the tent and sat. The Virgin took something out of the pack and crept over beside him.
He saw then it was Maria and Joe the Bush and she
had a bottle of whiskey and they were swigging it now
and laughing and after a while Joe whispered something.
She smiled, and put her head in his lap. Mickey closed
his eyes. There was a terrible noise of animals and
humans squealing, shrieking together like the pigs at
Clonfad and something in his head was saying: Help of
the weak, Refuge of Sinners, Comforter of the Afflicted,
but the noise got louder and above it clearly he could see
her beautiful head in Joe's lap and Joe was holding it

when suddenly Joe was shouting: "Christ" and then "Oh Christ, Christ, Christ, Christ" and pushed her from him. She spat, picked up the bottle of whiskey and drank till it was empty. She looked round and at him with lost eyes, a sag in her mouth, her face blotched, her hair a dirty frizz like old Maggie Greggan of the Gullet. There was a smell from them like the smell in Connolly's boarsty, so strong he could hardly breathe. He tried to get up. He couldn't. The smell got worse and began to smell like corruption and death and he couldn't breathe now at all because the smell was so bad and he was retching and then he was sitting up in bed choking and crying.

The stars were gone. In the corner of the loft Joe the Bush was asleep, his mouth open like a black hole in a grey stubble. It made him feel sick to look at Joe. He thought for a while, got up and strapped what he had into a blanket, emptied a box of clippings into a cardboard bin and went down the ladder. Grey light in the flagged yard. The slates of a disused bakery showed rain; church, houses, streets and fields seemed huddled, condemned. He washed at a tap in the yard. The water splashed on pocked cement and ran away down a blind gully that went under the dripping apple trees. He carried the cardboard box to a bare patch beside a plum tree and set fire to it. As it burned he dropped everything from the wad keeping only his Mother's memorial card. He watched the flames twist and warp and said aloud, "I'd like to be dead and buried, yes that's a fact". When the papers were ash he went back to the yard and looked up at the stucco house and read the words on the wall;

CAFE ROMA
Snacks, Fish Suppers, Accommodation.

A black plastic sewage pipe came down the middle of the house, past her open window with its blue curtains.

"I'll not think," he said, "I'll go."

Then he turned to climb the pipe. It was wet and slippery. He went down the stone staircase to the basement and got in the scullery window. Up then to the street hall with the arched doorway, big photographs, the table and two chairs. Up again the rubbernosed staircase to the upper landing with its one high window looking north. There was brown lino on the floor, a big green plant in a brass pot. Five doors. That was hers, open. He could see the blue curtains, her school uniform on a chair. He went in. She was deep asleep, breathing easy, beautiful as any picture he ever saw:

"Impure."

Her eyes opened:

"Impure," he shouted, "dirty."

She got up on elbows. He could hear himself but wasn't sure what he was saying. Then he was trembling and crying and muttering. Maria was startled. She felt no fear just pity, and shame.

"Mickey, I'm sorry. Please. Don't. You're shouting, you'll wake them. Please go, please."

"Impure, dirty, dirty, dirty."

Then Mr. Digacimo was standing in the room in pyjamas, the hair he combed carefully across his pate hanging down over one ear. Mickey was muttering:

"God Almighty's Mother, a bitch fit for any mongrel, dirty, impure."

Mr. Digacimo took his arm.

Maria said:

"Please Papa, he means nothing, he's upset."

Mickey pulled away and left the room. He saw Mr.
Digacimo on the landing in an overcoat. He heard her
say something that sounded like Police. He went out the
back door to the yard, put the strapped blanket on the
handcart and pushed it up the entry to the street.

"I'll not think, I'll go."

He went out the west road heading for Leitrim. He
heard a man say once there was nothing left in Leitrim
now but bare mountains, empty houses and the bones of
sheep. The hedges gave way to a straggle of whins. He
looked back and down. The town was gone in a smore
of rain. She too would die in his mind and be forgot,
like when a body died. Later there were cars, trucks
and vans; children on a school bus looked out pointing
and laughing. He went up a branch road. He would find
his way through side roads and lanes. There was no going
back. Tired he sat on a ditch and looked at the country,
the sun lost in clouds, thousands of crows flying somewhere, over dark lakes, November again, a thin wind,
and the fields sodden.

An old man came up the road driving two bony cows.
He had a fag-coloured stubble and smoky eyes, a
withered face like his father's:

"Where are you going with the handcart, son?"

"Leitrim."

"Where to?"

"I don't know."

The old man stared. Mickey got up and said, "I must
go." The old man said nothing, then spat and called:

"Good luck to you, son, and Leitrim."

Later he would pray when he could think easy. As long as you had God and his Blessed Mother it was no odds where you were going, or when you got there. He must keep to that and burn all else from his mind: that was truth. Then he said aloud:

"My heart is broken, that's the truth; my love is dead, that's a fact."

MUSIC AT ANNAHULLION

She put her bike in the shed and filled a basket of turf. Curtains still pulled across Teddy's window. Some morning the gable'd fall, and he'd wake sudden. Course you had to pretend to Liam Annahullion was very special. "See the depth of them walls" ... "Look at that door; they don't use timber like that now" ... and "feel that staircase, solid, made to last." Bit of a dose the way he went on; sure what was it only a mud and stone lofted cottage, half thatched, half slated, with a leaning chimney and a cracked gable.

"The finest view in Ireland," Liam said a hundred times a year. High to the north by Carn rock it was fine in spring and summer, very fine, but all you ever saw from this door in winter was the hammered out barrels on the hayshed, the rutted lane, and a bottom of rushes so high you'd be hard put at times to find the five cows. Liam went on about "the orchard" at the front put down by their grandfather, Matt Grue: a few scabby trees in the ground hoked useless by sows, a half acre of a midden, but you couldn't say that to his face.

One night Teddy said, "Carried away auld cod: it's because he owns it."

"Shush," Annie said, pointing upstairs.

"A rotten stable, it'll fall before we're much older."

"We grew up here, Teddy."

"Signs on it we'll all die here. They'll plant it with trees when we're gone."

"It's home."

"Aye."

Teddy talked like that when he came in late. He drank too much. His fingers were tarry black from fags, the eyes burned out of his head. Even so you could look into his eyes, you could have a laugh with Teddy. She called up the stairs as she closed the kitchen door.

"Teddy, it's half-eleven."

"Right."

He gave a brattle of a cough and then five minutes later shouted down: "Is there a shirt?"

"Where it's always."

"It's not."

"Look again."

She listened.

"Get it? In the low drawer?"

"It was under a sheet."

"But you've got it?"

"I got it."

"Thanks very much," Annie said to herself. She hooked a griddle over the glow of sods to warm a few wheaten scones. She could maybe mention it quiet like, give it time to sink. He might rise to it after a while maybe, or again he might know what she was up to and say nothing. He was always low over winter, got it tight to pay Liam the three quid a week for board and keep. In the summer he had cash to spare, on hire through the country with a 1946 Petrol Ferguson, cutting meadows, moulding spuds, buckraking, drawing corn shigs to the thrasher. Sometimes he was gone a week.

"Knows all the bad weemen in the country," Liam once said. "Got a lot to answer for, that bucko."

Teddy came down and sat at the north window under

an empty birdcage, his elbows on the oilcloth. A tall stooped frame. He ate very little very slowly, put her in mind often of some great grey bird; a bite, a look out the window, another bite. "You were up at Reilly's?"

"We'd no butter."

"Who was there?"

"George McAloon."

"Wee blind George?"

"He's not that blind."

Teddy lit a cigarette and looked out. He could see Liam stepping from ridge to ridge in the sloping haggard. The field had earthy welts running angle ways, like the ribs in a man's chest, hadn't felt the plough since the Famine or before.

"Anyone else?"

"Only Petey Mulligan the shopboy. He kep' sayin' 'Jasus' every minute to see poor George nod and bless himself, and then he winked at me, much as to say 'mad frigger, but we're wise' . . . too old-fashioned by half."

Teddy was quiet for a minute and then said: "Religion puts people mad."

"No religion puts them madder."

He thought about this. He hadn't confessed for near forty years, lay in bed of a Sunday with rubbishy papers Liam wouldn't use to light fires. Sometimes they had bitter arguments about religion and the clergy. Liam and Annie never missed Mass.

"It's a big question," Teddy said.

Annie filled a tin basin from the kettle.

"I saw a piana at Foster's."

"Aye?"

"In the long shed at the back of the garden."

"What's it doin' there?"

"They've put a lot of stuff out."

"What kind?"

"Horsetedder, cart wheels, pig troughs, beehives, auld churns, a grass harrow, stuff like that."

"Useless?"

"Less or more."

"Over from the auction."

"Must be."

"Odd place to leave a piana."

"The very thing I thought."

After a moment she said, "It looks very good, shiny with two brass candle-sticks, like the one in the photo."

"Auld I'd say?"

"Must be."

"The guts of fifty years."

"And maybe fifty along with that."

Teddy went to the door and looked out. Annie said to his back, "Pity to see a thing like that going to rack and loss."

"If it's worth money," Teddy said, "some fly boy goin' the road'll cob it ... maybe it's got no insides or it's rusted or seized up some way, must be something wrong with it or it would have gone in the auction."

"If it come out of Foster's it's good, and it could come at handy money."

Teddy looked round at her. "Who'd want it?"

Annie shrugged.

"You want it, Annie?"

"A nice thing, a piana."

"Everyone wants things."

Teddy looked through stark apple trees towards the

wet rushy bottom and the swollen river; rain again today.

"Who'd play it?"

"A body can pick out tunes with one finger, the odd visitor maybe, and you could put flowers on top of it, light candles at special times."

Teddy was picking at his teeth with a tarry thumb: "When one of us dies Annie?"

"Christmas, Easter, times like that."

He went on picking his teeth with the tarry thumb.

"It's a bit daft, Annie."

"Is it?"

There was a silence and Teddy looked round; when he saw her face he said, "Don't go by me, but it's a dud I'd swear."

"I'd say you're right."

He took his cap from the top of the wireless.

"I'll see if there's letters."

"Tell Liam there's tay."

Annie saw him cross the yard, a scarecrow of a man, arms hung below his knees. Teddy wouldn't bother anyway. A Scotch collie bitch circled round him, yapping and bellycrawling. Guinea hens flapped to the roof of a piggery. She could see Liam blinding potholes in the rutted lane. Even in winter scutch grass clung to the middle ridge. Teddy stopped for a word; hadn't much to say to each other that pair, more like cold neighbours than brothers. Teddy went on down the road. Two years back Liam had put the post box on an ash tree near the gate ... "to keep Elliot the Postman away from about the place."

"What's wrong with him?" Teddy had asked.

"Bad auld article," Liam said.

"What way?"

"Handles weemen, or tries to, in near every house he goes to, anyway he's black Protestant."

Teddy let on he didn't understand. "Handles weemen? What weemen?"

Liam got redder.

"He'll not put a foot about this place."

Annie thought about Joe Elliot, a rumpledy wee fellow, with a bate-in face, doggy eyes, and a squeaky voice. No woman in her right mind could let him next or near her without a fit of the giggles, but there was no arguring with Liam. He was proud and very private. Four or five signs about the farm forbade this and that. A "Land Poisoned" sign had been kept up though there hadn't been sheep about Annahullion for twenty years. When stray hounds crossed the farm Liam fired at them. Every year in the *Anglo-Celt* he put a Notice prohibiting anyone from shooting or hunting.

"Jasus," Teddy said, "thirty wet sour acres and maybe a dozen starved snipe, who's he stopping? Who'd want to hunt or shoot about here? There's nothin' only us."

Near the bridge there was a notice "Fishing Strictly Forbidden". The river was ten feet wide, the notice nailed to an alder in a scrub of stunted blackthorn that grew three yards out from the river bank. When the water was low barbed-wire under the bridge trapped the odd carcass of dog and badger; sometimes you could see pram wheels, bicycle frames, tins and bottles. Liam once hooked a pike on a nightline. She had cooked it in milk. It tasted strong, oily, Teddy wouldn't touch it:

"I'd as lief ate sick scaldcrows, them auld river pike ates rats and all kinds of rubbish."

Annie found it hard to stomach her portion. She fed the left-overs to the cat. Teddy swore later he saw the cat puke. Liam was dour for days. She heard him crossing the yard now and began pouring his tea; he blessed himself as he came across the floor, pulling off the cap.

"Half-eleven I'd say?"

"Nearer twelve," Annie said.

Liam nodded and sucked at his tea.

"You could say mid-day."

"Next or near, you could say that."

Liam shook his head. Every day or so they had this exchange about Teddy.

"I'm never done tryin' to tell him," Annie said. "I get sick hearin' myself."

"It's a pity of any man, he couldn't be tould often enough or strong enough."

"True for you," Annie said, and thought how neither of them ever dared a word, let alone hint. Teddy was his own man, paid steady for his room, helped about the yard or farm when he felt like it. Liam sucked his teeth. They were big and a bad fit, put you in mind of a horse scobing into a sour apple. He was squatter than Teddy, sturdier, slate-coloured eyes and tight reddish skin. He smiled seldom and no one had ever heard him laugh. Sometimes Annie heard him laugh alone about the yard and fields.

"Same as the Uncle Eddie," Liam said, "lazy and pagan and you know how he ended. In a bog-hole ... drunk ... drownded."

Crabbed this morning, better leave it till evening. "Teddy said you remarked a piana at Foster's."

Oh God, Annie thought and said, "I saw it from the road."

Liam ate another scone before he said, "Scrap."

"I'd say."

"Whole place was red out at the sale. Piana must have been lyin' about in a pig house or some of them auld rotten lofts."

"That's what Teddy said, a dud."

"He's right about that anyway."

And that's that, Annie thought. Soon they'd all be pensioned, maybe then she could buy the odd thing. It was put up to her to run the house on the milk cheque. It could be a very small one in winter. She made up by crocheting, anything but approach Liam. All afternoon she thought of the piano. In the end she found herself crying as she kneaded bread. "Yerra God," she thought, "I'm goin' astray in the head . . . an auld scrap piana, an' not a body in the house fit to play, and here I am all snivels over the head of it." She blew her nose and put it out of her mind.

It was dark when Teddy got back. He smelled of whiskey and fags and his eyes looked bright, Liam didn't look up from the *Anglo-Celt*.

"Your dinner's all dried up," Annie said.

"No odds," Teddy said.

Liam switched on the wireless for the news. They all listened. When it was over Teddy said: "I saw your piana, I made a dale for it."

"Ah you're coddin', Teddy!"

"It's out of tune."

"That's aisy fixed."

"Woodworm in the back."

"You can cure that too."

"There's a pedal off."

"What odds."

From the way Liam held the paper she could tell he was cut. God's sake couldn't he let on for once in his life, his way of showing he kept the deeds. Teddy winked.

"Who sould it?" Liam asked.

"Wright, the Auctioneer. It was forgot at the sale, hid under a heap of bags in the coach house."

"Cute boy, Wright."

"He's all that."

"How much?"

"Two notes, he give it away."

"You paid him?"

"He's paid."

"That's all right," Liam said and went out.

They heard him rattling buckets in the boiler house.

"Pass no remarks," Teddy said. "If you want a thing, get it. What's he bought here all his years but two ton weight of the *Anglo-Celt*, one second-hand bird cage that no bird ever sang in, and a dose of holy pictures."

"Horrid good of you, Teddy," Annie said.

"Ah!"

"No, it was," Annie said. "If you'd waited to chaw it over with Liam you'd be that sick hearin' about it you'd as lief burn it as have it."

"Liam's a cautious man."

Next day Teddy took the tractor out and went off

about three o'clock. Annie lit a fire in the parlour. It led off the kitchen at the end of the staircase. It was a long, narrow room smelling of turpentine, damp, and coats of polish on the parquetry lino. The white-painted boards, ceiling and wainscoting was yellow and spotty. Like the kitchen it had two windows at either end, a black horsehair chaise-lounge in one, a small table with a red chenille cover and potplant in the other. Two stiff armchairs faced the painted slate fireplace. On the mantelshelf there was a clock stopped since 1929, a china dog, and a cracked Infant of Prague. Annie looked at the photograph over the shelf: Teddy with a hoop, Liam wearing a cap and buttoned britches. Her mother had on a rucked blouse, a long skirt with pintucks at the bottom, high boots and gloves, and that was her with a blind doll on her mother's knee. Their father stood behind looking sideways. At the bottom of the photograph "McEniff, Photographer, Dublin Road, Monaghan 1914" ... some fairday long ago, no memory of it now. The rough-faced man and the soft young woman buried. She was now twenty years older than her mother was then, and she thought now how her mother in her last sickness had kept raving: "the childer, the childer, where are my childer?" She remembered saying "This is me; Annie, one of your childer." Her mother had looked at her steady for a minute, then shook her head. Course she was old, dying of old age.

It was dark when they sat down to tea and Liam said, "Long as he's not drunk ... and lyin' in some ditch under the piana. That would be a square snippet for the *Celt*."

"He'll be all right," Annie said.

No noise for an hour but wind in the chimney, the hiss of thornlogs through turf, and the crackle of Liam's paper. She began to worry. Supposing he did cross a ditch, get buried or worse over the head of it. Then she heard the tractor, and went to the door. A single light was pulsing on the bonnet of the old Ferguson as it came into the yard. Teddy reversed to the front door and let the buck-rake gently to the ground. He untied the ropes and put the tractor away. Annie tested the keyboard in the dark windy yard. There was an odd note dumb. Guinea hens cackled and the collie bitch barked. Liam was watching from the door.

"What's wrong with them?"

"Damp," Annie said. "Nothing a good fire won't mend." It was heavy, the castors seized or rusted.

"Like a coffin full of rocks," Liam said.

"Time enough," Teddy said. "No hurry."

They had a lot of bother getting it into the kitchen, Liam wouldn't let Annie help.

"Stand back woman, we're well fit."

It seemed very big in the kitchen. Teddy sat down and lit a cigarette. Annie took down the Tilley lamp and went round the piano. Made from that thin shaved timber; damp had unstuck some of it. That could be fixed. The keys had gone yellow but the candle-sticks were very nice and the music stand was carved. God, it was lovely. She lifted the top lid and looked down into the frame. She could see something ... a newspaper? She pulled it out, faded and flittered by mice. Liam came over.

"That's an auld one," Teddy said from the hearth.

"The 7th November, 1936," Liam read.

"The weight of forty years," Annie said.

From where he was sitting Teddy could read an ad:

WHAT

LIES

AHEAD

FOR

YOU

Why not make the future certain?

"What's in it?"

Liam had put on his glasses ... "A Cavan man hung himself in an outhouse."

"Aye?"

"Last thing he said to his wife was 'Will I go to Matt Smith's or get the spade shafted?' ... and the wife said 'Damn the hair I care but the childer have wet feet ... don't come back without boots'."

Liam looked up. "Then he hung himself."

"God help her," Annie said. "Women have a hard life."

"God help *him*," Liam said.

"Safer lave God out of it," Teddy said.

"I must have bought that paper and read that maybe ten times ... and it's all gone ... forgot ... Do *you* mind it, Annie?"

"No."

"You, Ted?"

"It's like a lot of things you read, you couldn't mind them all."

Liam put the paper aside. "Better get this thing out of the way."

He went to the parlour door, looked at it and looked

...ack:

at the piano. The two last steps of the staircase jutted across the parlour door. It was made from two heavy planks, each step dowelled into place. The whole frame was clamped to the wall with four iron arms. "None of your fibby boxed in jobs," Liam often said. "That's solid, made to last." He went to the dresser, got a ruler, measured, folded the ruler and said: "Won't fit."

"It'll be got in some way," Annie said.

"How?"

"Let's try and we'll know."

"If it doesn't fit, it doesn't fit. Damn thing's too big."

Teddy took the rule and measured.

"We might jiggle it in," he said, "it's worth a try."

"Won't fit," Liam said.

Annie made tea and watched for an hour, measuring, lifting, forcing, levering, straining, Liam getting angrier and redder.

"For Christ's sake, don't pull agin me."

"Where are you goin' now, up the friggin' stairs?"

"What in the name of Jasus are you at now?"

Finally he shouted, "Have you no wit at all, the bloody thing's too big, the door's too small, the staircase is in the way, it won't fit or less you rip down them stairs."

Annie tried not to listen. Teddy kept his voice low, but he was vexed and lit one fag off the other.

"Maybe we could strip her down," he said, "and lift in the insides, build her up again in the room."

"Maybe we could toss the sidewall of the house," Liam said, "and drag her through, that's the only way."

They said nothing for a while and then Annie said, "I suppose it'll have to go out again?"

"Where else," Liam said.

They got it out the door again and half lifted, half dragged it to the turf shed. Two castors broke off. The thrumming and jumble of notes set the guinea-hens clucking and flapping in the apple trees.

Liam went to bed early. Teddy sat at the hearth with Annie and drank more tea.

"It's only a couple of quid, Annie."

"No odds," she said.

He looked at her. He felt a bit of an eejit; maybe she did too.

"What odds what people say."

"I don't give tuppence what people say ... never wanted a thing so bad, dunno why, and to have it in the house."

"If you're that strong for a piana, we'll get one, the same brass candlesticks, one that fits."

"No."

Teddy looked at her again. If she'd come out straight and say what was in her head; women never did. They never knew rightly what was in their heads.

"Two quid is nothing, Annie."

"I told you, it's not the money."

Teddy sat a while at the fire.

"I'll go up."

He paused half way up the stairs. "It's only scrap, Annie, means nothin'."

"I know."

Annie dreamed that night that Liam had hung himself in the turf shed. Teddy cut him down and they laid him out in the parlour. She looked at the awful face on the piano, and then the face of the little boy in the photograph, and knelt. She felt her heart was breaking, she wanted to pray but all she could do was cry. "What are you cryin' for, Annie?" Teddy was standing in the parlour door. "Everything ... all of us ... I wish to God we were never born."

When she woke up it was dark. She lit a candle, and prayed for a while. It was almost light again when she fell asleep. That morning she covered the piano with plastic fertiliser bags. The guinea-hens roosted on it all winter. Near dark one evening in February she saw a sick rat squeeze in where the pedal had broken off. By April varnish was peeling off the side. One wet day in July Teddy unscrewed the brass candlesticks. On and off she dreamed about it, strange dreams that made her unhappy. It was winter again and one evening she said, "I'm sick to death lookin' at that thing in the turf shed. For God's sake get shut of it."

She watched Teddy smash it with an axe. In ten minutes the rusted steel frame lay in the hen mess of the yard like the carcass of a skinned animal. Teddy slipped the buck-rake under it and drew it out of the yard. From under the empty birdcage Liam watched through the kitchen window. "No wit, that man," he said. "Always bought foolish. His uncle Eddie was identical."

CANCER

TODAY THERE WAS an old Anglia and five bicycles outside the cottage. Boyle parked near the bridge. As he locked the car Dinny came through a gap in the ditch: "Busy?"

"From the back of Carn Rock and beyont: it's like a wake inside."

For a living corpse Boyle thought.

"How is he?"

"Never better."

"No pain?"

"Not a twitch ... ates rings round me and snores the night long." Boyle imagined Joady on the low stool by the hearth in the hot, crowded kitchen, his face like turf ash. Everyone knew he was dying. Women from townlands about had offered to cook and wash. Both brothers had refused. "Odd wee men," the women said. "Course they'd have no sheets, and the blankets must be black." "And why not," another said, "no woman body ever stood in aither room this forty years." At which another giggled and said, "or lay". And they all laughed because Dinny and Joady were under-sized. And then they were ashamed of laughing and said "poor Joady cratur" and "poor Dinny he'll be left: that's worse". And people kept bringing things: bacon and chicken, whiskey and stout, seed cake, fresh-laid eggs, wholemeal bread; Christmas in February.

In all his years Joady had never slept away from the cottage so that when people called now he talked about the hospital, the operation, the men who died in the ward. In particular he talked about the shattered bodies brought to the hospital morgue from the explosion near Trillick. When he went on about this Protestant neighbours kept silent. Joady noticed and said: "A bad doin', Albert, surely, there could be no luck after thon." To Catholic neighbours he said: "Done it their selves to throw blame on us" and spat in the fire.

It was growing dark at the bridge, crows winging over from Annahullion to roost in the fibrous trees about the disused Spade Mill.

"A week to the day we went up to Enniskillen," Dinny said.

"That long."

"A week to the day, you might say to the hour. Do you mind the helicopter?" He pointed up. "It near sat on that tree."

Boyle remembered very clearly. It had seemed to come from a quarry of whins dropping as it crossed Gawley's flat. Like today he had driven across this Border bridge and stopped at McMahon's iron-roofed cottage. Without looking up, he could sense the machine chopping its way up from the Spade Mill. He left the car engine running. Dinny came out clutching a bottle of something. The helicopter hung directly over a dead alder in a scrub of egg bushes between the cottage and the river. Dinny turned and flourished the bottle upwards shouting above the noise: "I hope to Jasus yis are blown to shit." He grinned and waved the bottle again. Boyle looked up. Behind the curved, bullet-proof shield two pale urban faces stared down, impassive.

"Come on, Dinny, get in."

He waved again: a bottle of Lucozade.

Boyle put the car in gear and drove North. They could hear the machine overhead. Dinny kept twisting about in the front seat trying to see up.

"The whores," he screeched, "they're trackin' us."

On a long stretch of road the helicopter swooped ahead and dropped to within a yard of the road. It turned slowly and moved towards them, a gigantic insect with revolving swords. Five yards from the car it stopped. The two faces were now very clear: guns, uniform, apparatus, one man had ear-phones. He seemed to be reading in a notebook. He looked at the registration number of Boyle's car and said something. The helicopter tilted sharply and rose clapping its way towards Armagh across the sour divide of fields and crooked ditches. Boyle remained parked in the middle of the road, until he could hear nothing. His heart was pumping strongly: "What the hell was all that?"

"They could see we had Catholic faces," Dinny said and winked. There was a twist in his left eye. "The mouth" McMahon neighbours called him, pike lips set in a bulbous face, a cap glued to his skull. Boyle opened a window. The fumes of porter were just stronger than the hum of turf smoke and a strong personal pong.

"It's on account of Trillick," Boyle said, "they'll be very active for a day or two."

"You'll get the news now."

Boyle switched on the car radio and a voice was saying: "Five men in a Land Rover on a track leading to a television transmitter station on Brougher Mountain near Trillick between Enniskillen and Omagh. Two B.B.C.

officials and three workers lost their lives. An Army spokesman said that the booby trap blew a six-foot deep crater in the mountainside and lifted the Land Rover twenty yards into a bog. The bodies of the five men were scattered over an area of 400 square yards. The area has been sealed off.

Boyle switched off the radio and said: "Dear God."

They passed a barn-like church set in four acres of graveyard. Dinny tipped his cap to the dead; McCaffreys, Boyles, Grues, Gunns, McMahons, Courtneys, Mulligans; names and bones from a hundred townlands.

"I cut a bit out of the *Anglo-Celt* once," Dinny said, "about our crowd, the McMahons."

"Yes?"

"Kings about Monaghan for near a thousand years, butchered, and driv' north to these bitter hills, that's what it said, and the scholar that wrote it up maintained you'll get better bred men in the cabins of Fermanagh than you'll find in many's a big house."

Boyle thumbed up at the graveyard: "One thing we're sure of, Dinny, we'll add our bit."

"Blood tells," Dinny said, "it tells in the end."

A few miles on they passed a waterworks. There was a soldier pacing the floodlit jetty.

"Wouldn't care for his job, he'll go up with it some night."

"Unless there's changes," Boyle said.

"Changes! What changes. Look in your neighbour's face; damn little change you'll see there. I wrought four days with Gilbert Wilson before Christmas, baggin' turf beyont Doon, and when the job was done we dropped into Corranny pub, and talked land, and benty turf, and

c

the forestry takin' over and the way people are leavin' for factories, the pension scheme for hill farmers and a dose of things: no side in any of it, not one word of politics or religion, and then all of a shot he leans over to me and says: 'Fact is, Dinny, the time I like you best, I could cut your throat.' A quare slap in the mouth, but I didn't rise to it; I just said: 'I'd as lief not hear the like, Gilbert.' 'You,' says he, 'and all your kind, it must be said.' 'It's a mistake, Gilbert, to say the like, or think it.' 'Truth,' he said, 'and you mind it, Dinny'.''

He looked at Boyle: "What do you think of that for a spake?"

They came to the main road and Moorlough: "Are them geese or swans," Dinny was pointing. He wound down his window and stared out. On the Loughside field there seemed to be fifty or sixty swans, very white against the black water. Boyle slowed for the trunk road, put on his headlights.

"Hard to say."

"Swans," Dinny said.

"You're sure?"

"Certain sure."

"So far from water?"

"I seen it before on this very lake in the twenties, bad sign."

"Of what?"

"Trouble."

The lake was half a mile long and at the far end of it there was a military checkpoint. An officer came over with a boy soldier and said "Out, please." Two other soldiers began searching the car.

"Name?"

"Boyle, James."

"Occupation?"

"Teacher."

"Address?"

"Tiernahinch, Kilrooskey, Fermanagh."

"And this gentleman?"

Boyle looked away. Dinny said nothing. The officer said again: "Name?"

"Denis McMahon, Gawley's Bridge, Fermanagh."

"Occupation?"

"I'm on the national health."

The boy beside the officer was writing in a notebook. A cold wind blowing from the lake chopped at the water, churning up angry flecks. The officer had no expression in his face. His voice seemed bored and flat.

"Going where?"

"Enniskillen," Boyle said.

"Purpose?"

"To visit this man's brother, he's had an operation."

"He's lying under a surgeont," Dinny said.

The officer nodded.

"And your brother's name?"

"Joady, Joseph, I'm next-of-kin."

The boy with the notebook went over to a radio jeep. The officer walked away a few paces. They watched. Boyle thought he should say aloud what they were all thinking, then decided not to; then heard himself say: "Awful business at Trillick."

The officer turned, looked at him steadily for a moment and nodded. There was another silence until Dinny said: "Trillick is claner nor a man kicked to death by savages fornenst his childer."

The officer did not look round. The boy soldier came back from the jeep and said everything was correct, Sir. The officer nodded again, walked away and stood looking at the lake.

Dinny dryspat towards the military back as they drove off. " 'And this gentleman!' Smart bugger, see the way he looked at me like I was sprung from a cage."

"His job, Dinny!"

"To make you feel like an animal! 'Occupation' is right!"

Near Lisnaskea Dinny said: "Cancer, that's what we're all afeerd of, one touch of it and you're a dead man. My auld fella died from a rare breed of it. If he went out in the light, the skin would rot from his face and hands, so he put in the latter end of his life in a dark room, or walkin' about the roads at night. In the end it killed him. He hadn't seen the sun for years."

He lit a cigarette butt.

"A doctor tould me once it could be in the blood fifty years, and then all of a shot it boils up and you're a gonner."

For miles after this they said nothing, then Dinny said: "Lisbellaw for wappin' straw,/Maguiresbridge for brandy./Lisnaskea for drinkin' tay,/But Clones town is dandy/ . . . that's a quare auld one?"

He winked with his good eye.

"You want a jigger, Dinny?"

"I'll not say no."

Smoke, coughing, the reek of a diesel stove and porter met them with silence and watching. Dinny whispered: "U.D.R., wrong shop."

Twenty or more, a clutch of uniformed farmers, faces

hardened by wind, rutted from bog, rock and rain, all staring, invincible, suspicious.

"Wrong shop," Dinny whispered again.

"I know," Boyle said, "we can't leave now."

Near a partition there was a space beside a big man. As Boyle moved towards it a woman bartender said: "Yes?"

"Two halfs, please."

"What kind?"

"Irish."

"What kind of Irish?"

"Any kind."

Big enough to pull a bullock from a shuck on his own Boyle thought as the big man spat at the doosy floor and turned away. Dinny nudged Boyle and winked up at a notice pinned to a pillar. Boyle read:

Linaskea and District Development Association
Extermination of Vermin
1/- for each magpie killed.
2/- for each grey crow killed.
10/- for each grey squirrel killed.
£1 for each fox killed.

Underneath someone had printed with a biro:

For every Fenian Fucker: one old penny.

As the woman measured the whiskies a glass smashed in the snug at the counter end. A voice jumped the frosted glass: "Wilson was a fly boy, and this Heath man's a bum boy, all them Tories is tricky whores, dale with Micks and Papes and lave us here to rot. Well, by Christ, they'll come no Pope to the townland of Invercloon, I'll not be blown up or burned out, I'll fight to the last ditch."

All listening in the outer bar, faces, secret and serious, uncomfortable now as other voices joined: "Your right, George."

"Sit down, man, you'll toss the table."

"Let him say out what's in his head."

"They'll not blow me across no bog; if it's blood they want then, by Jasus, they'll get it, all they want, gallons of it, wagons, shiploads."

"Now you're talking, George."

The big man looked at the woman. She went to the hatch, pushed it and said something into the snug. The loudness stopped. A red-axe face stared out, no focus in the eyes. Someone snapped the hatch shut. Silence. The big man spat again and Dinny said: "I'd as lief drink with pigs."

He held his glass of whiskey across the counter, poured it into the bar sink and walked out. Boyle finished his whiskey and followed.

In the car again the words came jerking from Dinny's mouth: "Choke and gut their own childer. Feed them to rats."

He held up a black-rimmed nail to the windscreen.

"Before they'd give us *that*!"

"It's very sad," Boyle said, "I see no answer."

"I know the answer, cut the bastards down, every last one of them and it'll come to that, them or us. They got it with guns, kep' it with guns, and guns'll put them from it."

"Blood's not the way," Boyle said.

"There's no other."

At Enniskillen they went by the low end of the town, passed armoured cars, and the shattered Crown buildings. Outside the hospital there were four rows of cars, two police cars and a military lorry. Joady's ward was on the ground floor. He was in a corner near a window facing an old man with bad colour and a caved-in mouth. In over thirty years Boyle had never seen Joady without his cap. Sitting up now in bed like an old woman, with a white domed head and drained face, he looked like Dinny's ghost shaved and shrunk in regulation pyjamas. He shook hands with Boyle and pointed at Dinny's bottle: "What's in that?"

"Lucozade," Dinny said.

"Poison."

"It's recommended for a sick body."

"Rots the insides; you can drop it out the windy."

"I'll keep it," Dinny said, "I can use it."

Boyle could see that Dinny was offended, and remembered his aunt's anger one Christmas long ago. She had knit a pair of wool socks for Joady and asked him about them.

"Bad wool, Miss," he said, "out through the heel in a week, I dropped them in the fire."

She was near tears as she told his mother: "Ungrateful, lazy, spiteful little men, small wonder Protestants despise them and us, and the smell in that house ... you'd think with nothing else to do but draw the dole and sit by the fire the least they could do is wash themselves: as for religion, no Mass, no altar, nothing ever, they'll burn, they really will, and someone should tell them. God knows you don't want thanks, but to have it flung back in your teeth like that it's ..."

"It's very trying, Annie," his mother said.

And Boyle wanted to say to his aunt: "No light, no water, no work, no money, nothing all their days, but the dole, fire poking, neighbour baiting, and the odd skite on porter, retched off that night in a ditch."

"Communists," his aunt mocked Joady, "I know what real Communists would do with those boyos, what Hitler did with the Jews."

"Annie, that's an awful thing to say."

There was a silence and then his aunt said: "God forgive me, it is, but ..." and then she wept.

"Because she never married, and the age she's at," his mother said afterwards.

Joady was pointing across a square of winter lawn to the hospital entrance: "Fornenst them cars," he said, "the morgue." His eyes swivelled round the ward, "I heard nurses talk about it in the corridor, brought them here in plastic bags from Trillick, laid them out on slabs in a go of sawdust on account of the blood. That's what they're at now, Army doctors tryin' to put the bits together, so's their people can recognise them, and box them proper."

The old man opposite groaned and shifted. Joady's voice dropped still lower: "They say one man's head couldn't be got high or low, they're still tramping the mountain with searchlights."

"Dear God," Boyle said.

"A fox could nip off with a man's head handy enough."

"If it came down from a height it could bury itself in that auld spongy heather and they'd never find it or less they tripped over it."

"Bloodhound dogs could smell it out."

"They wouldn't use bloodhound dogs on a job like that, wouldn't be proper."

"Better nor lavin' it to rot in a bog, course they'd use dogs, they'd have to."

"Stop!"

Across the ward the old man was trying to elbow himself up. The air was wheezing in and out of his lungs, he seemed to be choking: "Stop! Oh God, God, please, I must go ... I must ..."

Boyle stood up and pressed the bell near Joady's bed. Visitors round other beds stopped talking. The wheezing got louder, more irregular, and a voice said: "Someone do something."

Another said: "Get a doctor."

Boyle said: "I've rung."

A male nurse came and pulled a curtain round the bed. When a doctor came the man was dead. He was pushed away on a trolley covered with a white sheet. Gradually people round other beds began to talk. A young girl looking sick was led out by a woman.

"That's the third carted off since I come down here."

"Who was he?" Boyle asked.

"John Willie Foster, a bread server from beyont Five-mile town, started in to wet the bed like a child over a year back, they couldn't care for him at home, so they put him to 'Silver Springs', the auld people's home, but he got worse there so they packed him off here."

"Age," Dinny said, "the heart gave up."

"The heart broke," Joady said, "no one come to see him, bar one neighbour man. He was towld he could get home for a day or two at Christmas, no one come, he

c*

wouldn't spake with no one, couldn't quit' cryin'; the man's heart was broke."

"Them Probsbyterians is a hard bunch, cauld, no nature."

There was a silence.

"Did he say what about you Joady? . . . the surgeont?"

"No."

"You asked?"

" 'A deep operation,' he said, 'very deep, an obstruction,' so I said 'Is there somethin' rotten, Sir, I want to know, I want to be ready?' 'Ready for what,' says he and smiles, but you can't tell what's at the back of a smile like that. " 'Just ready,' I said.

" 'You could live longer nor me,' says he."

"He hasn't come next nor near me since I've come down here to the ground . . . did he tell yous anythin?"

"Dam' to the thing," Dinny said.

And Boyle noticed that Joady's eyes were glassy.

There was a newspaper open on the bed. It showed the Duke of Kent beside an armoured car at a shattered customs post. On the top of the photograph the name of the post read "Kilclean", Boyle picked up the newspaper, opened it and saw headlines: "Significance of bank raids"; "Arms for Bogsiders"; "Failure to track murderer"; "Arms role of I.R.A."

He read, skipping half, half listening to the brothers.

"In so far as ordinary secret service work is concerned, could be relied on and trusted . . . under the control of certain Ministers. Reliable personnel . . . co-operation between Army intelligence and civilian intelligence . . . no question of collusion."

"Lies," Joady said to Dinny, "you don't know who to

believe." His voice was odd and his hand was trembling on the bedspread. Boyle didn't want to look at his face and thought, probably has it and knows. Dinny was looking at the floor.

"Lies," Joady said again. And this time his voice sounded better. Boyle put down the paper and said: "I hear you got blood, Joady."

"Who towld you that?"

"One of my past pupils, a nurse here."

"Three pints," Joady said.

Boyle winked and said: "Black blood, she told me you got Paisley's blood."

Joady began shaking, his mouth opened and he seemed to be dry-retching. The laughter when it came was pitched and hoarse. He put a hand on his stitches and stopped, his breathing shallow, his head going like a picaninny on a mission box.

"Paisley's blood, she said that?"

"She did."

"That's tarror," he said, but was careful not to laugh again. Boyle stood up and squeezed his arm: "We'll have to go, Joady, next time can we bring you something you need?"

"Nothin'," Joady said, "I need nothin',"

Walking the glass-walled, rubber corridor Boyle said: "I'll wait in the car, Dinny."

Dinny stopped and looked at the bottle of Lucozade: "We could see him together."

"If you want."

The surgeon detached a sheet of paper from a file, he faced them across a steel-framed table: "In your brother's case," he was saying to Dinny, "it's late, much, much, too late." He paused, no one said anything and then the surgeon said: "I'm afraid so."

"Dying?"

"It's terminal."

"He's not in pain," Boyle said.

"And may have none for quite a while, when the stitches come out he'll be much better at home."

"He doesn't know," Dinny said.

"No, I didn't tell him yet."

"He wants to know."

The surgeon nodded and made a note on a sheet of paper. Dinny asked: "How long has he got, Sir?"

The surgeon looked at the sheet of paper as though the death date were inscribed: "Sometime this year ... yes, I'm afraid so."

The Anglia and bicycles were gone now. It had grown dark about the bridge and along the river. Boyle was cold sitting on the wall. Dinny had been talking for half an hour: "He was never sick a day, and five times I've been opened, lay a full year with a bad lung above at Killadeas; he doesn't know what it is to be sick."

Raucous crow noise carried up from the trees around the Spade Mill, cawing, cawing, cawing, blindflapping in the dark. They looked down, listening, waiting, it ceased. "He knows about dying," Boyle said.

"That's what I'm comin' at, he's dyin' and sleeps twelve hours of the twenty-four, ates, smokes, walks, and for a man used never talk much, he talks the hind leg off a pot now, make your head light to hear him."

He took out a glass phial: "I take two of them sleeping caps every night since he come home, and never close an eye. I can't keep nothin' on my stomach, and my skin itches all over; I sweat night and day. I'll tell you what I think: livin's worse nor dyin', and that's a fact."

"It's upsetting, Dinny."

It was dark in the kitchen: Joady gave Boyle a stool, accepted a cigarette, and lit it from the paraffin lamp, his face sharp and withered: a frosted crab.

"Where's the other fella gone?"

"I'm not sure," Boyle said, "he went down the river somewhere."

Joady sucked on the cigarette: "McCaffreys, he's gone to McCaffreys, very neighbourly these times, he'll be there until twelve or after."

He thrust at a blazing sod with a one-pronged pitch fork: "Same every night since I come home, away from the house every chance he gets."

"All the visitors you have, Joady, and he's worried."

"Dam' the worry, whingin' and whinin', to every slob that passes the road about *me* snorin' the night long, didn't I hear him with my own ears ..."

He spat, his eyes twisting: "It's *him* that snores not *me*, him: it's *me* that's dyin', *me*, not him ... Christ's sake ... couldn't he take a back sate until I'm buried."

He got up and looked out the small back window at the night, at nothing: "What would you call it, when your own brother goes contrary, and the ground hungry for you ... eh! Rotten, that's what I'd call it, rotten."

HERITAGE

HE STEPPED BACK as the pigeon shattered through the dairy window. For an instant he saw the brown outstretched wings of the hawk, the yellow flouted eyes. It swerved sharply left with a screech, cutting under the archway, up over the beech copse in line with the orchard towards the border river. He was holding the dead pigeon as his mother and Maggie Reilly crossed from the porch, his mother's mouth a question mark, Maggie's face fat, flat and curious.

"There was a hawk after it," he said.

"God help it," his mother said with pitying eyes.

He left it on the dairy window.

"God made it."

"Poor hunted cratur," Maggie said.

His mother touched the plumage. "These days every sound fright's me."

She had a grey dress on for service. Maggie had green Sunday buttons sewn on her Monday coat, a floppy brown woollen that covered her fourteen stone.

"I'll have your milk in ten minutes Maggie, I've cans to collect."

"No hurry, Eric."

Blister, his father's mongrel hound appeared from somewhere and ran from the yard, the pigeon in its mouth.

"Nature's cruel too," Maggie said.

Eric watched them walk towards the house. Maggie

had two children by different men, and lived in the office section of a disused creamery.

"A proper Papist hedge whore," George said often to his mother. "You should get shut of her, Sarah."

"Indeed I should," his mother said.

Maggie worked at other farms and helped out odd times with house parties at Inver Hall. Apart from harmless news his mother liked to hear, she was a good worker and likeable.

He went out under the stone archway. The rutted laneway, dry now in summer had a thick tuft of scutch down its spine. On a stricken ash in the middle of the orchard the hawk perched in rigid silence. Eric stood and looked. It stared back sullen. He clapped his hands sharply. It fell from the branch, swooped across the lane, upwards from the rolling fields and stout ditches of Drumhowl.

He followed its flight towards Shannock and Carn Rock, a dim, hidden country, crooked scrub ditches of whin and thorns stunted in sour putty land; bare, spade-ribbed fields, rusted tin roofed cabins, housing a stony faced people living from rangy cattle and Welfare handouts. From their gaunt lands they looked down on the green border country below watching, waiting. To them a hundred years was yesterday, two hundred the day before.

"A rotten race," George said, "good for nothin' but malice and murder; the like of Hitler would put them through a burnhouse and spread them on their sour bogs and he'd be right, it's all they're fit for."

The lane sloped steeply to the county road. He walked by the orchard and beech copse planted by his grandfather in 1921 to block off the view of the Fenian South. He could see through the grey-lichened trunks the slate coloured river winding through thick rushy bottoms past Inver Hall and Church towards Lough Erne. A week ago he had watched a gun fight between British soldiers and gunmen across the river in the Republic. He saw one gunman hit and dragged away by two others. His mouth was dry for hours after. Every other day this last few years their windows rattled from explosions in nearby towns and villages. Now since he had joined the U.D.R. the thing had got ugly. Three men he knew were dead, two U.D.R., one Catholic policeman. To-night when he put on his uniform his mother would be near tears. Every day when they talked about land, neighbours or cattle prices, they were thinking something else. He was a big target. He could be got handy. Death spitting from a gap or bog, a sharp bend in the road, a cattle mart or shop counter, a booby trapped pad between townlands, or blown asunder on the tractor drawing turf from Doon forest, where it seemed dark now in July. Anywhere, anytime, a clash to the head or body, brain shattered, his name in a news-reader's mouth :

"This evening in South Fermanagh, Eric O'Neill, twenty-one, a part time member of the U.D.R."

Where and how it happened, along with oil shortages, strikes and rumours of revolution. T.V. coverage, a vast Protestant attendance. The *Impartial Reporter* would give it two full pages with photographs, his father, George, Sam and Joe Robinson carrying the coffin, his mother supported by neighbours at the graveside. More hatred but he'd be gone from it. Forgot in a week except for Rachel and the family.

As he approached the milk stand he could see a label tied to the can handle. A reject? Then he noticed the envelope, black edged. Inside printed with red marker pen he read:

ERIC O'NEILL   U.D.R.   DRUMHOWL
BORN 1952
DIED ?
GET OUT ... OR BE GOT LIKE CROZIER   R.I.P.

He felt more anger than fear. Even now as he stood they could be watching ten fields away or further, in a hedge, up a tree. He put the note in his pocket, grasped the churns, jumped the low ditch and walked up the back of the hedge, keeping out of sight of the road, through the orchard into the yard. He brought the cans straight to the dairy. As he loosened the lids to let air circulate, he noticed his hands were shaking like an old man's. He was sweating. "I'm a coward," he thought. He took out the note and read it again. "R.I.P." a sick, cruel touch that. One by one he thought of his Catholic neighbours from Drumhowl to Carn Rock, tried to imagine them writing this ... all hard working people. Martin Cassidy the only active man in politics, a Civil Rights man; open and manly, respected by both sides.

Maggie came across the yard pushing her bicycle, a milk-can in one hand for two pints of milk, part payment for the work she did. She followed him into the byre.

"You tend them well, Eric, great cows God bless them."

She said this every day, or something like it. She understood the work that went into the feeding, cleaning and milking of twenty-three cows, the awkward calvings, calf scours, sudden deaths. She looked at him now with clear kind eyes, but of another race and creed, who might by now have decided on the time and place of his death. Eric hunkered to attach a milk bucket.

"You can't tell what they're thinking," George said "never, ever."

Straightening, he looked down at the four claws of the machine, the milk pulsing into the bucket.

"You're not talking to the people this morning, Eric."

"Sorry, Maggie."

He looked round. It was almost as if she knew. When she dropped her voice he listened carefully, looking straight into her eyes.

"Something to tell you, Eric," she was saying.

"Yes?"

"A neighbour man." She stopped and looked at the bright cobbled yard.

"This neighbour man, he told me he heard three men in a pub in Arva."

"Yes?"

"Talkin' quiet. They had a list of names at a table."

Colour had come into her face. She was finding this hard to say. He looked away, Maggie went on:

"From where he stood this neighbour man, he saw your name."

"What sort of list?"

"I don't know ... he said they were young men, not country boys."

She stopped again. "Could be another Eric O'Neill."

"Me all right ... maybe your neighbour left this for me."

As she read the note her eyes filled, Eric watched. "What neighbour man, Maggie?"

"A good man, wouldn't say a cross word to a dog."

"Would he know the men with the list?"

"Never seen them in his life ... he said they sounded like Tyrone."

"The publican must know them?"

"I wouldn't know that, son."

"How do they get names? How do they know when I come and go?"

He could hear a sharpness in his voice. She was staring with dilated eyes.

"They'll shoot postmen next."

"Get out, son."

"Maggie, I was in uniform, that's enough."

He had known her since he was a child and had never seen her look frightened. She knew a man who knew men who carried guns and were prepared to kill. He was on their list and she had warned.

"I'd as lief die myself, Eric, as see you harmed."

"I know that, Maggie."

"Honest to God, I . . ."

"My worry, not yours ... it's a bloody mess."

Outside under the winch-gibbet on the byre gable he tapped two pints of milk from the cooler.

"What'll you do, son?"

She didn't hear him say "I'm still alive" because of their old Bedford revving in the lane as it approached the arched entry. He watched it bounce over the stone gulley into the sunlit yard. His father reversed into the open turf-shed, cut the engine and opened a newspaper. Before he could think to stop her Maggie was moving towards the van. She talked with his father through the side window. When she left, his father got out of the van. He stood looking towards the byre, then walked towards the back porch of the house. One way or another they'd have heard. Notes like this had to be shown to Dixon the Commandant; sooner or later they'd all know. Twenty-five U.D.R. men shot since he had joined, buried in parish graveyards, skulls and bodies smashed, married or single, in or out of uniform. He felt again a hatred for these hidden killers, the hatred he felt for rats; everywhere watching, waiting, in walls and ditches, dung heaps and gullies, following old ruts and runs, half blind, grubbing on filth, smelling out the weak, the crippled and the cowardly. Trap, cage, shoot, or poison, hunt them with terriers, ferrets or starving cats, and a month later they were back, scraping, clawing, gorging, no ridding the world of them.

"Thinking like George now," he thought. "Beginning to hate them, *all* of them." Maggie? Sam's wife Maisie?

He tried not to think, finished the milking and crossed to the house. Pulling off his rubber boots in the glass porch he could see the kitchen door slightly open, voices loud inside; his mother's shrill. Silence for a few seconds. He pushed the hall door open a little. Sunlight from the kitchen window on the freshly polished linoleum, hand-made rugs, two stiff chairs and a hallstand, photographs of his O'Neill grandparents, an embroidered sampler, and a mahogany wall clock above the wainscotting.

"You pushed him in, woman, get him out now."

"Cruel to say the like of that."

"True: a death warrant, and you might as well have signed it, you and your brother George."

His father's voice was quiet. It seldom changed tone. His mother said: "He asked to join."

"Made to feel a coward if he didn't; a gun, a uniform and the money's good, that's what you said ... what he's got for himself won't bury him. Half his pay it took to put lino on that hall."

"He gave that to me."

"And you look down on Maggie Reilly."

"You talk to me of her."

"She loves her bastard sons, you've driv one away, and set the other up for a cock-shot ... my sons."

In the silence that followed Eric could feel his heart knocking strongly at his ribcage.

"It's me you hate, you've hated me for years."

"I'd rather be dead than talk like this."

"Better dead, a coward like all your people."

When he heard his mother cry he pulled on his rubber boots, went out to the yard and stood at the gable of the house. Worse than fear, hearing them like that. The voices had stopped.

"Get out," Sam said when he was leaving four years back.

"It's home," Eric remembered saying.

Sam said, "This place! It's a prison, worse; no drink, no smoke, no dance, no love, nothing but work, work, work and the Rev. Plumm every Sunday. Trouble or no trouble, no man could live in this house and stay sane."

He heard the porch door open, saw his father cross the yard.

"Eric."

He moved from the gable. "Here."

His father moved to join him; taller, leaner, a lined face under a weathered hat, deepset eyes, a huntsman, farmer and tradesman who could read the time on the Post Office clock from the far end of the street in Five-miletown. He looked now at Eric very directly.

"Maggie told me."

"Aye."

"Your mother knows."

"You shouldn't have told her."

"She'd have heard."

"She'll go off her head."

"Been off it since Sam married and before."

Eric looked away, his father said: "You could leave till things quieten."

"In a hundred years? I'd as lief take my chance."

"You'll be got if you stay."

"Someone has to...."

"I don't want to bury you, son"

"Someone must fight."

"Who? Every second neighbour? American money? Gangs of street savages. There's a reason for all that and they can't all be locked up hung or shot, they'll come again, and again, and again 'till they get what they want, or most of it, the same the world over."

Eric was tempted to say "Like rats" but didn't.

"I should have stood my ground that night, put George out and sent her to bed and said No. I should have took a stand. Show us the note."

He watched his father read. Two days of stubble seemed greyer.

"The whole thing makes me sick."

He handed back the note: "We'd best go in."

At the table his mother sat, hair knotted up, scared eyes, her face white as eggshell. When Eric looked up she was staring straight at him, porridge and wheaten bread on the deal boards, silence but for the wall clock in the hall. Then his mother said:

"You blame me both of you."

Eric said: "I blame no one."

"Whispering outside."

"Talking," his father said, "we'll say it again if you want."

"Men tortured in back streets, butchered fornenst their wives and childer, all of us awake when a car stops at night or the dog barks, and you blame me 'cause you think someone should take a stand."

"What's he fighting for, woman, God and country? The Queen? I'll tell you what he's fighting for ... the big boys who splash more on week-ends whoring than he'll make in a lifetime, and good luck to their whoring I say, if there's goms who'll die to keep them at it; that's your cause, son, the one true God, pound notes, millions of them, and the men who have them don't care a tinker's curse who kills who as long as they keep their grip, and if that's a coward's talk, I'll stay one."

"That's something you read in your trashy paper."

"It's the truth, woman."

"From a liar ... and a hypocrite."

"Take care."

"You'll take what you get from Papist or Protestant ... you don't care, and never will ... tip your cap to money like anyone else and I'll not hear speeches 'bout big men and their rotten lives, when there's little men twice as rotten."

"Like George?"

"He's not cruel to his own kin ... you said things to me just now, John Willie, no man who calls himself a man should say to any woman, let alone his wife, things I'll not forget the longest day I live."

His father was looking fixedly at a point on the kitchen floor, his face rigid. He said quiet and cold:

"You'll live to know worse days, woman."

"God forgive you."

"And you."

She was beginning to break. "The child is frightened."

"I'm no child, Mother."

"You didn't know what you were doing."

His father said blunt. "You did, George did. He signed, took the oath, money, what odds who's wrong or right, we've been over this a hundred times."

"You don't care."

"If one neighbour in ten thousand wants to kill me or mine, I'll not hate them all for that one, and I don't hate someone I've never met."

"Please, Da."

"Maisie, your own daughter-in-law."

"Please."

He understood what his father was saying, he knew what his mother was feeling.

"You don't know right from wrong, woman, good from bad."

"You're one to talk."

"Say what you like to your brother and his Christian friends, I'll not hear it in my house."

"A sad day I ever stood inside it."

"Damn little you've ever done in it, but gripe and whine."

She left the table stumbling as she went up the stairs, her bowl of porridge untouched. When they heard the bedroom door close, his father said:

"Day's I'd pay to be shot by anyone, dead and done with this crabbed life."

"You shouldn't, Da."

"What?"

"Talk so hard."

"I have reason ... take a drink, crack a joke and it's the end of the world, never heard her laugh right in thirty years, and never seen her body and won't or less she dies first and I'm at the laying out."

"Don't."

"True ... I had land, a stone built house, after you two were born she'd all she wanted from me ... hates bodies, her own and mine ... even food, hates that, won't eat fornenst strange eyes ... the other end of stooping, and that's shameful. She could live on black bread, water, the bible and hating Catholics; that's enough to keep her happy, makes me sick. If I could pray to God odd times it's not her blind God or George's. He's got a lot to answer for."

Eric could not eat. His father did not look up when he said:

"I'll change."

Passing his mother's room he could hear crying. He knocked.

"Yes."

"Me." He went in.

"Close the door, son." Eric did as he was told.

"The cruel things that man says to me with his quiet voice. I'd as lief he'd shout or hit me."

"We all say hard things be times."

"He meant every word, God in Heaven, how could he say such things, let alone think them. I told Sam before he married her I wouldn't meet that girl or let her cross the door. I won't pretend about Papists, he hates me 'cause I tell the truth, he's afraid of that."

Eric had heard this so often it was difficult for him to reply. If he disagreed she wept; if he seemed to agree even by silence she used this against his father . . . "Eric agrees with me."

"Am I speaking the truth, son, answer me?"

He picked his words carefully. "You believe what you say is true, Mother."

"I tell no lies."

"I know."

"Say what's in your head."

"You're distressed, that bothers me more nor the note I got."

She kissed his hand. "I'll die if anything happens to you, Eric, and he'll blame me, we should leave, all of us."

"How?"

"Just go."

"Where?"

"Away from here, anywhere, if we go he'll have to go."

"Sell out?"

"Yes."

"He won't."

"You were whispering out in the yard."

"Mother, I'll go if you want but . . ."

"If you go, we all go, for good. I'll not stay and hear a son of mine called 'coward'. God I hate this house, these blind bitter fields."

"We'll talk again."

He kissed her forehead, went to his room and changed. When he came down to the kitchen his father was staring out of the window, the *Sunday People* open on the table. He picked up the paper and nodded at the door. As they crossed the yard his father asked:

"What's she on about?"

"The same."

"Maisie?"

As they neared the turf shed the bedroom window went up with a snap. They stopped. Eric turned.

"Say it loud, John Willie."

His father kept his back to the house.

"You'll die, man, I'll die, and the only son we can call our own will be murdered if we don't go!"

His father turned and said looking at the ground: "If you want to go, woman, go, I'm staying."

"And do what, man?"

"What you want."

"Cook and scrub, is it? Wash and scald? I worked all my days for you, for next nothin' and when I ask one thing for myself, for your son, you say 'no'."

"You've got *two* sons."

His father dropped his voice and asked Eric: "You want me to sell or go?"

"No."

"Don't whisper," his mother screamed, "talk loud."

"All right I'll talk loud ... I was born here, I'll die here."

"Keep your fifty rotten acres, bury yourself in them and your son, and don't blame me."

Then the squeal of the window pulleys as the window snapped shut. Father and son stood in the sunlit yard looking at the ground.

"On thing to be said for the grave, you lie on your lone in a box; small wonder men die young, it's a wonder to Christ more don't hang themselves or walk out. What'll she pray about this morning in Church eh? 'Love thy neighbour' is it?"

Blister came bounding round the side of the barn. John Willie opened the door of the old Bedford. The mongrel jumped into the back.

"I'm taking the van," he said. "You'll have to walk."

Eric went back through the glass porch and stood listening in the long narrow hall. The wall clock, a tap turned in the bathroom, a helicopter somewhere far north. There was a smell of polish and paraffin oil. He opened the front door. July sunlight and the rich odour of cut grass. He looked at his pocketwatch, went back to the hallstand and took two hymnals.

"Mother."

"Yes."

"The van's gone."

"I heard, what's the time?"

"Quarter to."

Waiting at the hallstand he read the glazed and framed sampler stitched by his mother in memory of her own mother.

FOR ABIGAIL HAWTHORNE. 1874–1938
STRENGTH AND BEAUTY ARE HER CLOTHING
AND SHE SHALL LAUGH IN THE LATTER DAY.
THE LAW OF CLEMENCY IS ON HER TONGUE.
HER CHILDREN HAVE RISEN UP AND CALLED HER
BLESSED ... HER HUSBAND AND THEY HAVE
PRAISED HER. FAVOUR IS DECEITFUL AND
BEAUTY VAIN. THE WOMAN THAT FEARETH
THE LORD? SHE SHALL BE PRAISED

Between a sundial and a floral corner her signature stitched over in black thread:

Sarah Hawthorne
October 1941

She came round the bend of the staircase white with anger in her good Sunday coat and hat.

"Away with his filthy paper. Hunt ... and stupid beer talk, anything but Church ... Where's he gone?"

"He didn't say."

"Some Papist hovel up by Carn, thinks they like him, 'cause he can patch their slates and fix guttering, they'd knife him quick as they'd look at him, he'll find that out yet."

She was so angry, so used to Eric's silence that they walked by a farm pass to the back of Inver Church, without exchanging another word. Eric was grateful for the silence. July meadows baled or ensiled, pale or dark green, uncut meadows on rising land a light fawn colour, cows and dry stock content on good pasture. Over by Cavan and the Quilca Mountains the sky was a darkish blue, but clear over the rock. It would be a good bright windy day.

Inver Church came into view as they topped a low drumlin, a small Romanesque block all spikes and parapets with one sharp spire to the front in two acres of burial ground, the family church of the Armstrongs, their mausoleum massive and dominating amongst plain weathered stones. Here his O'Neill grandparents were buried in the unkept grave. The Hawthornes' grave, his mother's people, had heavy protective railings around it forged by George. Even now in summer George kept it trim and neat with hedge clippers, particular, like his sister, to show evidence of Protestant order and privacy. He was waiting now at the stile in a dark suit topped by a white face and grey hair, uneasy, his head at an angle, a restive scaldcrow.

"Well?"

It was a rebuke and a question. Sarah answered: "He took the van."

George shrugged and sucked at his teeth: "How's Eric?"

"Alive, George."

His uncle's limestone eyes stared from under shag-black eyebrows, both stood aside to let his mother through the stile. George followed listening as his mother told about the note, Eric dropped back. Twice George looked around with bleak concern. He tended the collection plate: there would be no time for talking until after the service. They went up the left aisle and sat in a pew near the baptistry under a white marble plaque, shaped like a shield. At the eagle lectern the Rev. John Plumm was reading from the Bible:

D

"And there is no remembrance now of former things nor indeed of those things which hereafter are to come."

He paused and looked down at the half-full Church.

"All things in this time are mingled together, blood theft, murder, dissimulation, corruption and unfaithfulness, and men keep watches of madness in the night."

In front of the lectern on the outside of the front pew sat Colonel Norbert Armstrong, erect and grey alongside his wife. Behind him a fine-skinned American with steel-rimmed glasses wearing a Norfolk jacket. Both pews were filled with the house party from Inver Hall. His father said often:

"They go for curiosity, to hear ould Plumm rave on, they believe in nothin' but land, stocks and shares, and keeping things the way they are."

Years ago he said he had seen a party of them bathing nude by moonlight in the shallow artificial lake fed from the Border river. "Blind drunk," he said, "leppin' on each other, men and women, squealing like cut pigs, a wonder to God the half of them weren't drowned."

A week ago some Fenian wag hung a dated tourist poster on the main gates:

COME TO ULSTER FOR YOUR SHOOTING HOLIDAYS

and smeared across it in green paint:

UP THE PROVOS

There was a rumour once that the Colonel had interfered with the game-keeper's son, and squashed a case with money. His father half believed the rumour, his mother rejected it as:

"Foul Papist lies. It's what they want to believe about all our kind."

Every now and then the Colonel fired off letters to the *Irish Times* and the *Belfast Telegraph* about Law, Order, Violence and the lunacy of Paisleyism. George bought the *Protestant Telegraph* and liked Paisley.

"The I.R.A. wouldn't waste a bullet on the Colonel," he said once, but he tipped his cap as reverently as the next, and shod their hunters when requested at the Estate forge. The Rev. Plumm looked at the empty gallery on either side:

"If thou shall see the oppression of the poor, and violent judgements, and justice prevented in the province, wonder not at this matter, for he that is high hath another higher, and there are others still higher than these." Eric watched George across the aisle, a daw listening for worms.

"All human things are liable to perpetual change. We are to rest on God's providence and cast away fruitless cares. I said in my heart concerning the sons of men, that God would prove them, and show them to be like beasts. Therefore the death of man, and of beasts is one; and the conditions of them both is equal; as man dieth, so they also die, all things breathe alike; and man hath nothing more than beast; all things are subject to vanity. And all things go to one place; of earth they are made and into earth they return together."

The Rev. Plumm turned from the lectern. George got up and moved for the collection plate. All stood to sing, Miss Pritchard fingering the introductory phrases of Psalm three:

> Oh Lord, how are my foes increased!
> Against me many rise.
> Many say of my soul, for him
> In God no succour lies
> Yet thou my shield and glory art,
> The uplifter of mine head.
> I cried and from His Holy hill
> The Lord me answer made,
> I laid me down and slept, I waked;
> For God sustained me
> I will not fear though thousands ten
> Set round against me be
> Arise, O Lord; Save me, my God
> For Thou has struck my foes
> Upon the cheek; the wicked's teeth
> Hast broken by Thy blows
> Salvation surely doth belong
> Unto the Lord alone;
> Thy blessing, Lord, for ever more
> Thy people is upon.

Service over, the Rev. Plumm walked into the presbytery. The Colonel stood in the aisle to allow his guests out first, English mostly, Eric thought, over with a pack of otter hounds he had seen yesterday from the haggard, a mahogany trailer towed by a yellow Land Rover. When the house party had filed out the Colonel walked down the aisle glancing and nodding here and there. Tom and Ruth Robinson followed with Joe and the rest of the congregation. Rachel remained seated. Eric smiled at Tom Robinson, an arthritic old farmer with a strong face. He winked at Joe who scarcely nodded back. When the church was empty Rachel looked around. Eric went into the baptistry; she followed. Through the high Gothic window they could see the sunlit graveyard, George and his mother talking with Rachel's parents, Joe sitting by himself on a tomb slab smoking a cigarette. A fine boned narrow face like Rachel's, which seldom showed colour or emotion, the same cool eyes, hair like bleached deal, Joe's ruffled at the nape, his skin coarsened by work and weather. Miss Pritchard was playing something complicated. It was hard to talk with the sound of the organ. Rachel took his hand and said:

"I've got 'till tomorrow, night duty next week. Were you talking to Joe?"

"He looked worried."

She hesitated. "Last night they stopped me near Maguiresbridge, three of them in tunics and berets."

She was looking out at the graveyard.

"When they found I was Joe Robinson's sister one of them said 'We should eff her arseways, only she might like it', another showed me a pistol and said 'See this you black bitch, I'll ram it between your legs next time you, your brother or any of his like puts a hand on any of ours, and tell him from us we'll blow his effing brains out first chance we get'."

The words, and the quiet way she told it startled him more than if it had been screamed. The note in his pocket now seemed trivial; he could feel blood coming into his face. He said:

"They mean it."

"I know. I begged Joe all night to get out, he won't listen, will you talk to him, Eric?"

He shrugged.

"You can try."

"Your auld fellow's not fit to work, your place'd go
to rack without Joe, even if he did get out what would
he do? Where would he go?"

"Dig tunnels in Britain, anything; at least we could
sleep at night."

"I'm not leaving, and I got a note tied to a can this
morning."

"A note?"

"A warning."

"From them?"

"Who else?"

"Oh God."

The organ was pumping so loudly they were almost
lip-reading. They waited for the passage of music to
stop. On the baptistry wall on a large sheet of rec-
tangular bronze, there was an engraved account of the
Armstrong family, their arrival with King William,
battles, sieges, glory, death and reference to the "dis-
affected Irish". In this marble font under this window
both had been baptised in Christ to serve God and love
neighbours. All round the church walls heraldic inscrip-
tions, faded flags, sculptured guns, flutes, pipes, bayonets
and loving tributes to violent death in Gallipoli, Flanders,
Germany, North Africa.

"Catholics kneel under plaster saints," his father remarked once, "we sit with Christ under guns and
swords."

The Rev. Plumm came down the aisle dispensing a
nod towards the baptistry.

"Why do we come here?"

"It marks the week."

When the Rev. Plumm was gone Rachel said: "Let's go out."

From the arched entrance they saw groups of neighbours standing about exchanging news and views, George mouthing strongly with his mother and the Robinsons, an old Forge bellows, the hiss of iron in the cooling tub. As Rachel moved into the sunlight to join them, Eric said:

"I want a word with Joe."

He went over, handed him the note, and said: "Rachel told me about last night."

Joe read the note and handed it back without a word. He was looking across the river at the lime-washed Catholic church half a mile away, a plain stucco barn-like building, with a separate belfry, a white Madonna in a cave between the church and the curate's bungalow, a full congregation funnelling through the square porch spreading through their graveyard.

"Bees from a hive," Eric said.

"Wasps," Joe said.

"Any notion who stopped her?"

Joe shook his head.

"All Fenians round here, could be any of them."

"You believe that?"

"What odds what I believe or you ... they'll choose the time and place, pick us off, no chance to fight back."

"Unless we go."

"I can't."

"Nor me."

"Do your people know?"

"What?"

"About last night; Rachel?"

Joe shook his head. "They're worried enough."

Cars were beginning to move from the Catholic church park down to the border bridge, the sun throwing flashes of hostile light from windscreens as they turned up for Carn. Joe jerked his head towards the gaunt uplands.

"It's a jungle from here to the rock; they don't need phones, radios or helicopters; sneeze at the back of a ditch, they know who it was and why he was there; they know every move, we don't stand a chance."

True. It was what Eric had told Maggie two hours ago. A lot of men got notes and were still alive. There was no point in further talk. Eric asked:

"You goin' to the hunt?"

"What hunt?"

"Otter, some pack from across, come last night to the Inver crowd. My auld fella's goin'."

"In our house they're death on doing anything of a Sunday."

"So's my mother and George, we might as well walk after dogs as sit and worry."

"What time?"

"Three, at the Hall."

"I'll come if I can."

"Bring Rachel."

"She hates huntin'."

"Ask her anyway."

Eric went over to join the others. Old Tom Robinson was looking at the gravel, squat in his late sixties, his wife Ruth, a tall thin woman with a forlorn face, blinking against the light, watching Eric approach. His mother was touching her upper lip nervously, upset by what George was saying. Eric heard him rasp:

"If we don't do it to them, they'll do it to us, and that's the story to the bitter end."

Old Tom looked embarrassed. George looked at Eric: "Any man tries to slide out is no man."

"I'm not sliding out George."

His mother said: "He's not your son, George. . . ."

"More to me nor his own father. When it comes to the bit I can depend on him."

Old Tom said, "I'll run you up, Sarah."

"It's only ten minutes," his mother protested.

"Take the lift, mam," Eric said. "I'll walk."

He nodded at the Robinsons and Rachel and moved away.

George called, "Hould on, son, hould on."

Eric slowed, waiting.

"What's your hurry?"

Eric was tempted to say, "I don't want to listen to you George." He said nothing. Afraid of George, of his mother, afraid to pick between his mother and his father, afraid of Catholics, afraid to hate or love. It was from George as a child that he first heard about Catholics in the forge at Oakfield:

"I'll shoe no Catholic ass, my boot in his hole."

And some of the Protestant men in the forge took out their pipes and laughed. Others said: "You're an awful man, George."

But even as a child he knew they agreed with George. When a Catholic did bring work he was greeted with "Well?" or "What's wrong now?" or "What are you trickin' at this weather?" With Protestant neighbours he was courteous and helpful. "How's all the care, Bob?" No Catholics had come near his forge now for three

D*

years. He jerked his head towards the lime-washed church across the river.

"I'll say one thing for them, they're animals with balls, our side whines like Ruth Robinson ... what's the end of it to be at all, at all, at all. Whiners get their teeth kicked down their throats."

George slashed at a nettle on a neglected grave with his blackthorn.

"Have you lost your tongue?"

"You have all the questions and answers, George."

"I know my mind, son, and you know yours if you were let, your father doesn't give a damn, and your mother wants you out, am I right?"

"Out where? I took an oath George, I'll stick by it."

"Now you're talkin'."

From the stile, across a narrow humped field of thistle and ragwort lay George's forge, a low squat crypt separate from the slated house, three fine oak trees at the back, proof to passing poverty in second hand cars that Oakfield could grow sound hardwood.

"Come on up a while, we'll brew tay and talk."

Eric wanted to refuse but had no ready excuse. He nodded assent. Every day of childhood, summer and winter, on his way home from school he had called with George, running messages across the spongy river bottoms to Johnson's border shop, black green rushes so high he sometimes lost his way, always a reward for his trouble, a slice of bread and butter sprinkled with caster sugar. In this world of small fields and bogland he had loved and still did, this coarse bigoted man with his rasping voice. No matter how he spewed blind hatred, it was difficult to disengage from the past, to scrap old memories. The lane they walked on now was rutted by a thousand carts, the bramble shoots reaching half-way across as they did every summer.

"A good straight man," his mother said. "The best blacksmith in Ulster, afraid of nothing and no one."

"You're wrong," his father said, "he's afeered of everyone and everything, drinks every penny he gets and too mean to marry, and all that loud rough talk; thinks he hates Catholics, it's himself he hates, and I wouldn't fault him for that."

In the sepia light of the kitchen George wet strong tea from the black range. They faced each other across the blue checkered oil-cloth; on the wall smokey portraits of the Queen, Carson and Paisley, a row of faded sashes, a large drum sitting beside a disused dash-churn in one corner, alongside it a thick pile of *Protestant Telegraphs*. As a child the sound of the drum frightened Eric so much that he crept to his mother's bed at night.

"It's only uncle George with his drum," she whispered, "nothin' to be afeered of."

This last few nights ten townlands could hear him thumping at the dusk beside the iron scrap heap behind the forge. Next Thursday on the Twelfth at Fivemiletown, he would make it reverberate to the whole mountain. He took a sip of tea now from his mug and stared out the window, a welt on his left cheek where a mare had lashed it twenty years ago.

"Any man drives off a Sunday and leaves his wife walk to Service is a poor breed of man."

"He had cause maybe, in his own mind."

"What cause? What's he ever done for her or you?"

"Pay bills."

pound a week this thirty years, what's that now,
you son the farm would have been sold off long
know that, I know that."

"He works, George."

"Not real work, not like you or me."

"He helps, when he's home."

"When's that? Tinker, footer, travel, talk? Drink in
Papist houses, and doesn't give an ass's fart when his
first-born marries one of *them*, went to the weddin' in
their church, and your mother at home near astray in
the head, what sort of man's that?"

Eric moved from the table. "I'd as lief you didn't talk
this way George."

"Afeered of the truth, son?"

"He's my father."

"And Sam's?" George paused and added quietly; "and
more."

Eric said nothing for a moment and then: "You better
say what you mean, George."

"She's been abused, your mother, that's what I mean."

Odd times, maybe twice a year, his father went on
three-day benders. Twice in the last six months Eric had
collected him, once from a pub in Blayney, and last time
from a boarding house in Armagh. George drank every
day. He despised men who couldn't hold their drink,
and keep their feet.

"Don't you want to hear, son?"

Eric stared, he wanted to say yes and no.

"It's time you heard."

The limestone eyes jerked round from the window:
"That eegit son of Maggie Reilly's, that's your half-
brother . . . true."

It was like a sharp slap on the face from a cold heavy hand.

"You know what you're saying, George."

"I do. From his own mouth I got it eighteen years back, after the fair at 'skea. We both had a drop taken, I put it to him square, and he didn't deny it. I tould him then if I ever got hint of the like again I'd kill him stone dead and I meant it. That's why he hates me."

Maggie had been working at Drumhowl since he was born, and every week since he could remember. Eric tried to shape the question in his mind, George answered it before he could ask.

"Every man and woman for miles around knows, bar you, Sam and your mother, and she must half know, that's what has her the way she is."

Eric went to the small back window that looked north. He could see Robinson's Vauxhall coming down the steep lane from Drumhowl. Joe and Rachel? The whole country?

"You shouldn't have said that, George."

"Time you heard, son."

"Why tell it?"

"Cause you don't back her. Now you know what she suffered, still suffers, that fat sow waddling up every mornin' for her milk, workin' around the house, twice a week, sickens me to my stomach to think of it."

George got up and poured himself a measure of Bushmills whiskey.

"Don't take it too hard."

"I don't believe it, George."

There was a pause. The side of George's mouth went down a little. For a moment he seemed almost angry, then he turned with a shrug.

"Would I lie about a thing like that? Ask him, your father, tell him what I said, see what he says."

In the half circle of gravel before Inver Hall he could see about a dozen cars including their old Bedford. A speedboat bounced on the water about a hundred yards from the shore, two skiers making a pattern behind it. After dinner with his mother, he was evasive about checking a heifer. From her eyes he could feel she suspected. Had he said he was going to join the hunt at Inver she would have asked him not to go, and he would have agreed. Because of what George had told him this mild deception cut sharply. Her face was still in his mind. As he walked through the parkland he could see his father clearly now with local huntsmen and farmers on the stretch of lawn between the eighteenth-century house and the lake, wee Willy Reilly amongst them, wearing the silly knitted cap like a tea cosy he wore summer and winter. The stables and yard were separate from the house, the otter pack whimpering, scraping at the wrought-iron gates, like big rough-haired foxhounds.

Two-stepping down the granite steps in black Aran sweater, grey flannels and shabby tennis shoes, Colonel Armstrong came clapping his hands for attention, directing his voice to the local huntsmen:

"Sherry, tea and seed cake inside before we start, the hunt begins at three sharp."

The voice across the lawn seemed to cut the out-board to silence, the two skiers skimming ropeless towards the shallow gravel. There was hesitation for a moment, then simultaneous mutters.

"Dammit, that's nice?"

"Aye."

"Why not, sir?"

"That's a dacent notion."

Of the dozen local huntsmen three were Catholics including Willie Reilly. The Colonel said: "Dogs not of the pack should, I think, be kept on leash, or tied until we see how they behave."

More muttered agreement. Small boys and youths were left in charge of the dogs. The huntsmen moved towards the house, his father talking easily with the Colonel. He had the casual self-respect of a farmer tradesman working over thirty years through the country; tinker or gentry, Papist or postman, he was the same with them all, a man seemingly without worries. Robinson's Vauxhall was not among the cars. His father seeing Eric approach put up a long arm and pointed towards the house. Eric signalled back, but decided to wait for Joe. He watched the skiers tinkering at the out-board motor, till he heard the car. He was surprised and pleased to see Rachel beside Joe. She wound down the side window.

"Might as well see an otter killed before one of you get it."

"Is your father here?" Joe asked.

Eric nodded to the house. "Inside."

"Posh," Rachel said.

"Sherry, tea and seed-cake."

"Parlour or pantry?" Rachel asked.

Eric shrugged and smiled. She seemed petulant, looking at the skiers and the lake.

"Do we have to go in?"

"Unmannerly not to."

"Would they notice or care?"

"We'll go in," Joe said, getting out. "I like to hear them talk."

He walked towards the steps.

"Can't stand her," Rachel said.

"Who?"

"The Colonel's wife. . . . They'll put us down in some poke with a bottle of cooking sherry."

"They're all right," Eric said.

"With two thousand acres they'd need to be."

He had helped here at threshing as a boy. Armstrongs' arrogance was natural. It was the way they were bred, and the Colonel had obliged him in different ways, loaning him farm machinery and a Friesian bull. The flagged hall went the length of the house, a wide slow-raked staircase, walls hung with military portraits, and strong faced women; couches, odd shaped chairs and garden furniture round the walls, a central refectory table, decanters of sherry, tea cups and a canteen type tea pot with two handles. There were about thirty people in all, locals grouped separately in a corner baiting Willie Reilly. Joe had joined them. Eric could hear his father laughing. He paused with Rachel at a games table mid-way between the local group and some of the house party. The American with the steel-rimmed glasses was talking to the Colonel's daughter, beside them the Pack-master. He looked a bit like Harold Wilson. Then he saw Maggie Reilly coming out behind the staircase with a steaming steel container. As she walked to the table his father leaned towards her and said something. Maggie smiled. Eric felt suddenly embarrassed and uncomfort-able. His father's voice was easy and teasing at Willie Reilly:

"Thon wee brown bitch of yours, Willie, what happened her ear?"

"I et it," Willie said.

There was a burst of laughter. With his slightly mongoloid face, the stutter and blue knit beret, he was a natural target for yeomanry unease in gentry surroundings:

"What odds about her ear, she's got the best nose in the country."

Someone said: "She's very small, Willie, very small."

"Hardy, well bred, and fast, and she'll stick to the river, just you watch, not like some big auld mongrels I'll not mention."

Another said: "If an otter got a good grip on her, Willie, he'd pull her under."

"Would you think that, Petey?"

"I would, Willie."

"That big dog of yours John, what do you call him?"

"Blister."

"Aye . . . Blister . . . pity he's blind."

The laughter turned from Willie. Eric heard his father chuckle.

"He can see a mile off, Willie, and he can smell further."

"But will he hunt with the pack, John?"

"Ahead of them, Willie."

There was a slight burr in his father's voice. He had spent the morning in a pub somewhere. Eric felt a revulsion now he had not thought possible.

The Colonel was going around with a tray of sherries and a decanter, his wife following with a plate of cut seed cake. The Colonel asked Rachel:

"Sherry or tea, dear?"

"Sherry, please."

"Eric?"

"Tea, please."

The Colonel called over: "Tea here, Maggie."

Mrs Armstrong held out a plate of seed cake. She looked at Eric with unfocused, brown eyes and smiled as he took a slice of cake, then moved on to Rachel. Maggie came waddling over and filled Eric's tea cup. There was a slight tremor in his hand.

"You look awful worried, Eric?"

Rachel said: "He got a love letter this morning Maggie."

Maggie frowned and said: "Some playboy sent that, pass no remarks."

When Maggie moved away Rachel asked: "Are you all right?"

"Yes."

"What's wrong? Do you want to go out?"

"No."

Gradually the quickness of his heart slowed. The people in the hall seemed glazed. He sat on the side of an armchair, his teacup on the games table. Rachel leaned towards him and said quietly:

"I love you."

He looked at her and said: "And I you ... something come over me, I'm sorry."

"What?"

"Nothing, I'll tell you after."

The American was saying to the Colonel's wife: "Yes but the kill is a fact of nature, Harriet, and nature plays sick jokes on all of us, like blindness, right? Old age? War? Death?"

"Brother Rat St. Francis said, likewise Brother Otter."
She smiled oddly.

"Was he sane?"

"The greatest human being since Christ. Have you read
Chekhov's *Ward No. 6*?"

"No."

"About a doctor in an asylum who realises as he goes
mad that sanity is locked away and lunatics outside run
the world ..."

"Odd notion!"

"Probably true."

"You're joking, Harriet!"

"If they were in charge history might make more
sense!"

"History would end!"

"A consummation devoutly to be wished."

The American laughed. The Colonel was among the
locals again, refilling proffered glasses. He dropped his
voice and said to Eric's father:

"This Packmaster isn't over keen on local hounds
joining the pack; if dogs get out of hand some of you
may have to put them on leash or withdraw them, you
understand."

"Aye surely, Colonel."

"That makes sense."

"We're not here to spoil the sport," his father said.

Willie Reilly stuttered, "My wee bitch will hunt
with any pack, she'll stick with the best of them
Colonel."

"I hope she does, Willie."

"She's killed otters, and foxes and hares, and an auld

badger dog, big as a boar, that's what happened her ear."

"There must be a drop of the tiger in her, Willie."

Laughter caused all heads to turn in the direction of the locals.

"Yes'll not laugh when ye see her working."

The Colonel moved towards the Packmaster and had a word with him. He looked at his wrist watch and said:

"We'll have to make a start."

Locals and guests followed him towards the big double door. Only the Colonel's wife remained. She stood at the refectory table, with the same odd smile.

The iron gates of the yard were opened. The otter hounds came whimpering and whining on to the sloping lawn, smelling and snarling round local hounds. Blister stood rigid as the pack nosed warily round him. The Packmaster shouted something, the Whipmaster cracked his whip for order. As Rachel and Eric walked across the gravel to the lawn, Rachel asked:

"Do you want to tell me what got you inside?"

Eric was watching the dogs. "The auld fellow and Maggie Reilly."

There was a ten second silence before she said: "That's a long way back."

"How long have you known?"

"School, I didn't rightly believe it 'till I heard them at home one night."

She paused and looked up at him. "You never guessed?"

"Nothin' till George this morning."

"So?"

"My mother, she must know, and that one up every day about our place."

Rachel stepped up on to the grass and moved ahead of him. She turned. "Could happen to me."

"Could it?"

"Any woman . . . or you, like your father."

Eric shook his head. Willie Reilly was laughing and yapping with excitement. He had unleashed his wee brown bitch. She was making circles in a small area wagging her tail between her legs. The Packmaster was saying something to Willie.

"Because she's Catholic?"

"Maybe. I don't want to think about it."

"Don't, it's history now."

John Willie came over smiling, his hat cocked well back.

"Are you children going to talk or walk?"

Rachel asked: "Will we see any otters killed John?"

"You'll not see an otter, let alone a kill."

The horn sounded and John Willie moved away, the Whipmaster in the middle of the dogs, the Packmaster walking ahead with a steel-shod stave, the countrymen with ashpoles in their dark clothes and caps, coats tied with twine across their shoulders, the house party in colourful gear with an assortment of blackthorn and racing sticks. Now and then the Whipmaster called a dog by name . . . Elvis, Togo, Billy . . . all fanning out, the dogs setting a sharp walking pace. Where the lake narrowed to the river the hunt spread to both banks, the Packleader midstream wading haunch-deep, the Whipper on the northern bank, the otter hounds swimming, plunging, lapping water, testing otter holts, running up

and down shallow drains. Where the lake ended, the
river went in a slow curve for half a mile. All land north
of this was Armstrong land, reclaimed and in good
heart, a deep, bog loam, rye grass with tufts of coxfoot,
laid out in ten-acre divisions, a herd of over eighty cows
grazing in one division, a Friesian bull walking alert
through them. Wee Willie's brown bitch had left the
river following a hare scent. The bull came trotting
towards her, head lowered. She came back cowering to
Willie's heels.

"That wee bitch of yours, Willie, she'll kill a bull before the day's out."

General laughter from the locals as Willie said: "The
day's not done yet."

He kicked his dog sharply in the ribs. She ran off
yelping. The hunt paused to watch Willie running up a
ditch after her. Someone said:

"Between them they'll kill a hedgehog!"

The flat land sloped upwards, loamy hillock country,
rising sharply thereafter to the gaunt highlands left of
Carn Rock, thousands of acres planted with larch and
Sitka spruce. Eric saw the American looking up and
heard him say to the Colonel:

"It's Greek."

"It can be beautiful."

"How far does Inver go?"

"To the forest, ten townlands, but there's shooting
rights for some hundreds, some I've never stood in."

Rachel said to Eric: "Let's cross."

The river was knee-deep. They crossed to the southern
bank. The sun was high and hot. From this first bend
the narrow tributary of the Finn changed character,

snaking through boggy rush land, long weedy tendrils
waving in the brackish water, broken sedge and froth,
tins and plastic bags damned by a rusting barbed-wire
fence from bank to bank, the bric-à-brac of a river dump
used by the Grues of Annahullion, Catholics. The dogs
swam under the wire. The hunters got out of the
river to by-pass. The banks were now so steep they had
to stay in the river bed or walk the high verge watching
from a height. Rachel and Eric kept to the bank. A crane
hidden in an area of sedge and bulrushes flapped slowly
out, rising gradually, as though in slow motion towards
a scrub of alder and stunted thorn. Midstream, John
Willie waded alongside the Whipmaster. His eyes did
not follow the crane. He was watching Blister who
seemed to keep separate and now broke away swimming
strongly across a deep dark pool, towards a big leaning
forked ash tree cloaked with ivy. At the opening of the
fork he gave a screeching yowl partly dispensed by water
in his mouth. The otter hounds immediately gave tongue.
The horn sounded, all dogs swimming towards the fork,
scrabbling to get a grip on the bare tentacles of ash root.
The Whipmaster hunkered, slipping sideways down the
northern slope, thrusting himself towards the tree, a
terrier yapping at his heels. When he reached the trunk
he grabbed a root with one hand, the terrier by the
scruff of the neck and thrust it into the opening with
some rough word of encouragement that sounded like
"g'winn, g'inn". The terrier went into the hole. All
stood, the hounds frustrated at the opening were scrambling up again. The Packmaster followed by John Willie
waded chest-deep to the opening and listened, examining
the earth for tracks.

The Master shouted: "One here or was!"

All waited, watching. Nothing. The Whipmaster got up on the tree-trunk, held a branch of ash and jumped up and down on the sloping earth as best he could. Still nothing. Blister had left the pack and gone down the river hunting alone. The American's voice came from the far bank.

"Scent is an astonishing sense."

The terrier appeared at the opening, shaking a glossy river rat. Rachel giggled with relief. The rat went floating slowly down stream, twitching. Most faces registered disappointment.

"Not quite a trophy," said the American.

"There was an otter here," the Packmaster called up.

"Could be a quarter of a mile away by now," the Colonel said.

"I hope it's at Lough Erne," Rachel whispered and asked: "Why do they hunt them?"

"They eat trout."

"So do we. Have you seen one ever?"

"Twice."

"Killed?"

"No."

"What are they like?"

"Big water squirrels, brown fluffy fellows, whiskery, with bit tails."

"They sound nice."

"They are."

"Timid?"

"They'll fight if they have to, a whole pack, so they say."

Unseen by Pack or Whipmasters Blister had worked his way out of sight round another bend. John Willie

knew this but did not draw attention to it. The hunt
proceeded slowly. There were a lot of holts in this deep
section, men and hounds working back and across from
one holt to another.

Down river Blister gave tongue. There was a look
between Pack and Whipmaster. The hounds replied,
scrambling out of the river, bypassing a hundred yards'
stretch towards Blister's call. All running now, men,
women, huntsmen towards the bend. When they got
there it was an arched bridge, a car parked on it. A small
round man standing on the parapet waving his cap and
shouting something. All running now towards the bridge.
The man on the bridge was pointing down towards the
pond of a disused scutch mill. House party and hunters
crossed the bridge and got down into the shallow water
underneath. The man was saying:

"A big otter dog, by Christ he must weigh thirty
pounds or more, thon big hound dog of John Willie's
near caught him."

At the bridge the water was two feet deep, deepening
gradually as the pond widened. It was deeply ringed
with bulrushes, sedge and reeds. Anything moving
would be spotted. The mill-race was damned by three
old railway sleepers, the end of the pond a limestone
wall. The mill itself had been shattered last year by the
I.R.A., U.D.A. or British Army; no one quite knew or
at the moment cared. Under the bridge ten men had
now formed an underwater barricade of legs by standing
close together, moving slowly down the pond prodding
ahead with their ashpoles and iron-shod staves. About
half the otter hounds were in the pond swimming, the
other half hunting the fifty yard stretch of bank and

sedge on either side. With a sudden heart stop Eric saw a small brown head emerge in the sedge on the left bank. He was about to shout. Instead he nudged Rachel and pointed with a jerk of his head. Her mouth opened in wonder and pity; she whispered:

"Don't, Eric! Don't! Let it live, let it live."

As they watched the brown head submerged again. No one else had noticed.

From the cottage above the mill a small hunched figure came down towards the pond, through a half acre of flowering potatoes. Rachel asked:

"Who's he?"

"Dinny McMahon."

"He has a gun."

"I can see that."

"What's he doing?"

"Dunno."

They watched the figure pushing through the thorn ditch, stumping across a waste of egg-bushes, boortrees and brambles to the clearing at the edge of the pond where the dogs worked and the men and women watched. No one looked round until he aimed his gun at the water and splayed a blast of pellets through the swimming dogs. There were shouts from the men, screams from the women, yelps from a dog. All turned to look at the small man. He split his smoking shotgun, dropped the empty cartridge, put his hand in his pocket and inserted another cartridge. In the silence everyone could hear the click of the hammer going back. The Colonel walked out of the river to face the gunman. Only Eric and Rachel could see the two figures outside the cottage.

"Yes!?" His military voice, a rifle report.

"No," the little man said, his voice a hard Fermanagh rasp.

"What do you mean? No."

"That's what I mane NO ... Sorr. Colonel ... I mane go back to the bridge and round the other side."

"Who are you?"

"Here a thousand years, and the same again, McMahon, Daniel and this mill-pad is mine, it's my land you stand on, and I say 'No' to you, and all like you, and to any of my own race down there in that shuck with you, none while I breathe is goin' to go down this pad, no means no, and that's that."

"I see."

"I'm glad you're not blind, Sorr, I can see rightly too and I want to see you walk back that pad while I stand here."

An otter hound was whimpering on the bank licking at his flank which seemed bloody and shattered.

"Did you have to fire on the dog?"

"Ah Jasus, is it the poor cratur of a dog, slaverin' to rip a wee otter dog half its size?! Shite talk, Sorr, keep it for your guests at mess in the Hall."

The hounds had stopped hunting aware of human tension. The chain in the river had slackened. The four women present looked frightened. The Colonel unruffled, his voice iron hard asked:

"Is this the townland of Shanroe?"

"You're on it, Sorr, my part of it, all three acres."

"I have hunting and shooting rights for this townland and all the townlands from Inver to Corrawhinny."

"Is that a fact?"

"It is."

"Well I have shooting rights here in my two hands, that's how you got yours, and if you want now I'll show you how it works."

He raised his gun and aimed it directly at the Colonel's head. John Willie came up from behind the Colonel both arms outstretched, stepping between the Colonel and the gun.

"Ah now, Dinny, for Christ's sake!"

"Go back, John."

"Dinny, please listen . . ."

"You listen . . . John, go back, I'm tellin' you."

Eric felt a contraction in his stomach. The little man said:

"I've nothing against you or yours, John, I only want you and this man to get back to the bridge, and go down the far bank. From there on you can hunt to Enniskillen, you can kill all the otters in Ulster for all I care. What I say is plain and I mane it, and you better tell your friend, the Colonel, that."

John Willie turned and had a quick-whispered word with the Colonel. The Colonel said to McMahon:

"Do you understand what you are doing now?"

"Do I look a fool?"

The Colonel said nothing to this.

"If I were you, Sorr, I wouldn't think about police let alone mention them. It'd take one of her Majesty's buggerin' Regiments to shift me, you can go in God's good time, or now; if you don't I'll blow the head clane off your shoulders."

Again John Willie said something to the Colonel. For ten seconds that seemed like a minute the Colonel stared

coldly back at the two-barrelled gun, and the ugly
hunched little man with one eye closed. When he turned
to go back the chain in the river broke, going different
ways to the southern bank. The Colonel walked slowly
towards the bridge, his face impassive as a boot.

The Colonel's daughter looked very white and shaken.
She took his hand. He let her hold it for a moment. As
he moved towards the American he passed Sam Heuston
who had left the river and was walking towards Mc-
Mahon.

"I wouldn't," the Colonel warned.

"I will," Heuston said and then shouted suddenly at
McMahon: "There's one not afeered; I'll walk this river
bank and you'll shoot me dead before I quit: bluff!"

For a moment McMahon stared then spat: "Scaldcrows, weasels aye, and river rats, I'll honour *them* with
this." He tapped the barrel of his gun: "Not *you*, . . . let
the Colonel try again or the dogs and you'll see how I
bluff."

At the bridge the American said to the Colonel: "In-
teresting."

The Colonel asked John Willie: "Do you know him,
John?"

"Dinny McMahon, I do Sir, he's half-odd."

"A lunatic," the Colonel said. "We've hunted this
stretch before."

"Before 'sixty-nine," Courtney said.

Tony Courtney was a Catholic who trained gun-dogs
for the Colonel. There was a long pause and then the
Colonel said:

"Yes."

All faces fixed in suppressed anger or embarrassment

watched the small hunched figure, ignoring Heuston's taunts, walk back through the potato patch towards the cottage. The Colonel asked:

"Whose dog is grained?"

The Whipmaster said: "One of the pack."

"Better take it to the vet . . . whose car is this?"

The man who waved on the bridge said: "I'll take the dog, Sir."

The dog's leg was badly shattered. The Whipmaster lifted the dog into the back seat of the car and got in beside it. The car drove off. The rest of the pack were walking about the bridge, some still shivering with excitement, others looking intently up at the human faces. From a mass of bulrushes near the mill-race there was a brown splashy leap, a quick scrabble and the otter was over the rotting sleepers and swimming down the mill race towards the steel structure of the wheel. In a few seconds it would be in open river again and away. If anyone noticed apart from Eric they made no mention. The Colonel said:

"No point in standing about."

The Packmaster said: "Can't we walk down the left bank and hunt on?"

The Colonel said bluntly: "No. We'll go back, trailer the dogs and hunt Mullivam."

There were general murmurs:

"You're right, Colonel."

"Wouldn't plaze him."

Sam Heuston back from his confrontation said: "If I had my way I'd bury him alive and hunt on."

"I don't want talk like that . . ." the Colonel said.

"I don't want talk either," Heuston said, "I'd do it."

"Trivial . . ." the Colonel said . . . "we'll forget all this and go."

"I'll not forget it . . ." Heuston said.

Courtney and the other Catholic farmers looked very tense.

"I'm sorry," the Colonel said to Courtney.

With a glance he included the other Catholic huntsmen. Heuston said:

"I'm not sorry."

The Colonel said: "I'm not afraid to use a gun Sam, or face one, but I reject that sort of thinking."

He jerked his head towards the McMahon cottage: "You're talking his language."

Heuston said: "And look where it's got them, look where it's left us, twenty men on a bridge afeered to cross because of a wee man with a gun, afeered to tell police, for fear we'd be blown up or burnt out . . . you think about that, Colonel, hard, 'cause you'll have to sooner than you think."

He snapped his fingers, and walked off, followed by a mongrel hound. Joe said quietly to Eric:

"He'd get on well with your Uncle George."

Eric said: "They drink together."

John Willie came over and Rachel said: "For a moment I thought he was going to shoot."

John Willie shook his head and smiled.

"He's waited years for that, and he'll put in the rest of his life telling about it."

Rachel said: "It didn't look that funny from here."

"You two coming to Mullivam?"

Before Eric could answer Rachel said: "No."

Joe said as he left with John: "See you to-night, Eric."

"Right."

From the bridge they watched the hunt spread back up the river 'till it went out of sight. Rachel took the ash rod Eric had broken off on his way down the river and threw it into the water. They watched it float down and stop against the dam. Rachel said:

"Let's go home by the fields."

From Shanroe bridge to Tattnagolan was about four miles as the crow flies. They climbed across a wooden bridge into Sam Foster's farm, unreclaimed bottom land, sprit, rushes and rough tussocks growing from a heavy morass, snipe twisting and wheeling away as they walked, white clouds drifting north towards the fields under Carn Rock. They stopped at Foster's well, a clean stone arched well, white-washed with a glitter of gravel in the bottom, so clear they could see spiders and tiny creatures walking on the surface. As they were about to drink they paused and turned to look. From half a mile they could hear the great wing beats. Two swans came down the river from Inver, flying low over the mill, heads craned for Lough Erne. They stared as though they had never seen swans fly before.

"So beautiful," Rachel said, then added, "but so ugly . . . the world."

"You're not."

"How I feel is . . . the hunt, and that little man, a thing like that, I get sick with hate, fear or both."

They drank from a tin porringer, chained by its handle to the wall of the well. For minutes they sat in silence looking. Then Rachel said:

"At home I listened . . . I thought they're wrong my parents, because we had Catholic neighbours. I didn't want to hate them, and I didn't, but in the delivery ward in April some time they were mostly Catholics. I heard them talk, so coarse and stupid, holy magazines and rosaries and this fuzzy-headed priest going about blessing their labours and their babies, and the horrid way they sucked up to him." She paused: "Even I didn't hear what I heard at home, I couldn't live with them or work with them because ..." She paused again and shrugged ... "Last night those animals ... their husbands ... sons, brothers, cousins; they do hate us, you can feel it."

For a moment Eric was silent and then: "I've seen them look at me in streets, marts, I don't want to hate or kill any of them, but a body must do something when the thing's gone the way it has."

"Get out."

"I can't."

"If you don't, you'll ..."

"We can't run out, we're farmers. I love these fields."

"More than me?"

"We *made* this country, they *are* this country and know it, they won't rest 'till they bury us or make us part of themselves. Like you I don't want that, maybe that's why I joined, though I'm not sure now."

"We didn't ask to be born here, I don't want to stay here now."

"Nor me."

"Can I tell you something?"

"Anything."

"It's ugly."

"If it's about you it's not."

"It's ugly ... I was on night duty a month ago, infant

E

wards, all Catholics, in the middle of the night I thought . . ."

"Go on. . . ."

"I thought if I set fire to it they'd all be burned, about thirty less of them."

There was quite a silence before Eric asked: "Dreamt or thought?"

"Thought Eric, thought. I was tired, I wouldn't do it in a million years, but I did think about it, how I'd start the fire, make it seem accidental, and when I knew what I was thinking, I got so frightened I almost got sick. That's why I'm leaving after midwifery. We're sick Eric, they're sick, and we don't know what to do, I want to believe in God, I can't, I want to be happy, I can't . . . Look around, look, Eric, it's beautiful . . . you are too . . . you are!"

She looked intently at the nail of her left thumb and said: "You've never touched me ever, why?"

He was so startled when he realised what she meant, that he said without thinking: "It's wrongful."

"Yourself, have you touched yourself, ever?"

He heard himself mutter: "Of course."

He knew, without looking at her face, that her heart was thumping.

"Me too, more wrongful that, when we love each other."

He glanced up; her face was tense: "No, don't look away, Eric. I'm shy too. Along the river I thought, I'll talk today, say what's in my head, ask him, tell him, and . . ."

"I know."

"You don't because . . ."

"Yes I do. . . ."

She stopped suddenly. The questions had come cramped and awkward from her mouth that always had two answers where he could seldom stammer one. Her mind, quick and contrary seemed more frightening to him than her body, untouchable in the old Bedford smelling of pigs, or cinemas reeking of perfumed Jeyes Fluid. He had hardly ever kissed her without embarrassment and awkwardness, believing what his mother told him often.

"You say so little, Eric, I don't rightly know what you think."

"I don't rightly know myself."

"Then I'll ask again; you've never touched me, why?"

"It's for begetting. I believe that."

"And love?"

"In wedlock."

She shrugged and stood suddenly. "Let's walk."

He followed, angry with her, with himself. You could read up about politics, farming and veterinary, learn from experience and mistakes. What book could explain this girl to him or his mother. She was ahead of him, alongside a ditch of foxgloves and double-combed bracken, walking soft as a cat, her jeans clinging from ankle to knee. She turned and said:

"I shouldn't talk that way, it's too forward."

"Better than treacle talk, but I don't want to feel stupid: I want to understand."

"Only for you I'd hate men . . . all men, you make me feel special."

"You are."

"Far from it."

"To me, you are."

She was staring at him. Then she was crying. She took his hands and put them to her face. He could feel her kissing his hands.

"Why are you crying, Rachel?"

"I don't know."

The brindle heifer was not with the cows nor in the beech copse. He went to the Fortfield, three cowstepped acres topped by a circle of ash, thorn and hazel. The heifer was on her side pressing in a mass of nettles and docks, the forelegs and nose of the calf protruding. He spoke to her gently strapping his belt round the slimey forelegs. With a foot on her hinchbone he pulled steady for five minutes. The head slipped, coming inch by inch, tongue out. He rested, his body wet from tension. Another five minutes and the shoulders were clear, then the whole calf, slurping out. He slapped it sharply on the ribs, cleared its throat with his forefinger and stood it on splayed shaky legs. Then the heifer was on her feet, afterbirth sat on stone, and watched the calf nosing round till it found the warm udder, a teat to suckle. He wiped his hands with dockleaves. Birthsmell, rich warm and milky mixed with rank odour of nettles: and man hath nothing more than beasts. All things go to one place: of earth they are made; to earth they return together. But they knew nothing of love or hate, tithes or time, the packer's knife, the knacker's lorry. And what did he fear? Death? What differ when the body chilled, now of a sudden or slowly in a cockloft fifty years from now? And what did he think she had asked. Not much of this life as he knew it less of what comes after. Afraid more of living than dying. A coward's mind? Rightly or

wrongly it was what he thought. And love? The warm
secrets of her body which he feared to touch would
cool to clods with bones and rusted mountings; her
children, and her children's children walking the same
pad.

He left the calf suckling and walked the cows from the
river bottoms round the lower end of the housefield,
approaching the yard from the front of the house. His
mother came out in wellingtons to open the gate. She
would see his pants were wet from the river and ask.
Should he lie or tell? The truth would hurt; the lie more
deeply if she heard later.

"Were you in the sheugh, son?"

"I followed dogs with Joe and Rachel."

"A hunt?"

"Yes."

She helped him tie the cows.

"Was your father there?"

"Yes."

"Where is he now?"

"Up Mullivam way; we left after an hour."

She said nothing and went back to the house. Spooning
an egg at table he caught her eye.

"You said you were going to check the heifer."

"I was, she's calved, a white-head bull."

"You knew about the hunt, that's the same as a lie."

"Is it?"

"He's always lying. I don't believe a word comes
from his mouth and that hurts; you don't lie to someone
you feel for."

"No but ...."

"Do you, son?"

"No."

"I'd as lief you wouldn't hunt God's creatures of a Sunday or any day, but I wouldn't interfere, would I?"

"No," he lied and finished his egg in silence.

"Why don't you talk, son?"

"Thinking."

" 'Bout what?"

"What you said."

"Lies?"

"Aye, and Sunday . . . God's creatures."

He couldn't say what he thought. By ten-thirty he had to be in uniform, then drive with George to the U.D.R. Head Quarters at Lisnaskea. They would be stopping and searching cars 'till four in the morning. He drank his tea and looked out at the slow twilight:

"You think I am a hypocrite?"

"What?"

"You heard."

"Yes I heard, Mother."

"Because I pray but won't see her, Sam's," she paused dropping her voice before she said "wife."

Eric shrugged. She went on:

"It's wrongful I know, and I've prayed God to help me but . . . the children of my first born . . . Papists . . . and Maggie Reilly pleased to tell me there's another coming . . . God help him . . . I shouldn't say this but I think it . . . I'd sooner he was dead."

"You don't mean that, Mother?"

"There are things you don't know, son: the joke now is a good person . . . the world's gone bad . . we should beget as God intended work hard and pray . . . that's what I was taught: I believe it, I abide by it."

Eric found the contradiction painful. Very quietly he said: "And love our neighbour?"

"Those who murder! ... Only Christ himself could do that ... other ways I try to be honest ... kept my marriage vows, reared you boys and run this house for a man who used me unnatural from the start ... and false from the start."

It was time to go. Eric stood. When he had kissed his mother she said:

"I don't want to be the way I was this morning. Ever ... because I love you, son, and your father, as much as he hates me."

"He doesn't hate you."

"Worse ... he doesn't care."

It was near dark at Oakfield when George came out in uniform. He slumped in the front seat of the Bedford, thrusting a rifle between the seats. Eric put on parking lights and drove the twisting hump-backed lane towards the county road. In the soft, grey dusk there was a herd of cows on the road, Willie Reilly in front with a torch. He pretended not to recognise Eric's van. As the cows passed the man at the back moved towards the car. Cassidy. Eric wound down the window.

"Eric."

"Martin."

"How's George?"

"I know how I am and how *you* are!"

McMahon's stand at Shanroe bridge was already local legend. Eric could see Cassidy smiling in the faint light of the dash.

"I hear Willie's wee bitch disgraced him today?"

"Reilly's dog wasn't the only thing happened today," George said.

There was a moment of silence and then Cassidy said : "There's a bomb scare in 'Skea."

"How do you know that ?" George asked.

"Radio."

"We'd better move son."

As they drove away George said : "A cog in the murder gang, one of your Yankee mafia, I mind him bare foot, his auld fella out for hire, tricked his way into Protestant land."

"You don't know that, George."

"Catholic and Civil Rights, isn't he ? . . . Seen him two years ago on the platform in Derry with that wee whore Devlin. See the way he smiled. He's laughin' at us; every bomb that goes off, every man that's maimed or murdered, laughin' 'cause they think we're afeered. No balls, that's what they say to therselves. He knows who sent that note, knows where, when and how you'll be got, it's all linked : Rome, politics, America, gunmen. In Christ's name how did he get money to buy Protestant land and pay two prices for it, a back-hander to a crooked solicitor and some lundy to bid; and them cows ! The whole shute must come to near £30,000 !"

"Borrowed, he works hard, George."

"Murder money; they're diggin' graves for us night and day and we're standin' lookin' at them like the Jews in Europe; they've got their score to settle and they mean to settle once and for all; if we let them."

A scaldcrow feeding on the carcass of a run-over dog flapped away as they passed in the growing dark.

"We bate them before : we'll bate them again."

Two miles from Lisnaskea they could see flames and ragged smoke over the town.

"Cassidy's bomb," George said.

A British Army patrol stopped them. They showed their papers, a soldier said:

"One of your mates got it an hour ago."

"Where?"

The soldier called back to the radio jeep: "Where were the father and son got?"

A voice called back: "Tatnagone."

Eric's heart stopped. There were only three families in the townland of Tatnagone.

"Name?"

"Robinson."

Eric heard himself ask: "How?"

"Gunned in a car at the house; the son's dead."

Eric could feel his body shaking. He drove slowly into Lisnaskea past a burning supermarket, two fire brigades, black helmeted figures, the garish street, Saracens and shattered glass, debris, soldiers, a siren moaning, huddled groups in the doorways; people sweeping up glass, a draper's dummy headless in a shop window. George said:

"Someone must pay."

There were about a dozen cars at Robinsons, two black R.U.C. patrol cars, a U.D.R. jeep, and overhead a helicopter with a powerful beam scanning fields and ditches. As he got out of the van George said loudly:

"Mick Cunningham's car! What's he here for?"

"He lives two fields away," Eric said.

"What's he here for?"

"It's no time for shouting, George."

E*

Dixon the commandant said: "George, we don't want guns in a dead house, leave it in the van."

George made a kind of whining noise: "For Christ's sake what are guns for?"

Dixon said: "You take no gun, you can stand out here with your gun if you want!"

George handed his gun to another U.D.R. man. Dixon answered Eric quietly:

"About an hour ago Cunningham heard the shot and got on the 'phone, we were here in ten minutes."

"Old Tom?"

"In the head, unconscious; poor chance. Joe died outright."

Eric had seen this kitchen often in a dream, the black police uniforms, British soldiers, Ruth Robinson on a chair by the stove delirious with grief, two other neighbour women trying to comfort her, a superintendent taking notes. In a corner Mick Cunningham, a tall balding Catholic with a heron's neck and the eyes of a rabbit. Eric had bought a suck calf off him two years ago, a big, harmless fellow with a shrill voice. From where he stood Eric could see into the parlour, Joe's boots level with a pot plant in the window, Bryson the undertaker measuring. As he moved towards the parlour door he saw George edge like a coiled spring towards Cunningham. Whatever he said it was as though he had struck him in the mouth. Cunningham jerked a nod and moved sideways towards the front door. Eric paused to let Bryson out.

The body was sheeted, Rachel sitting on a stiff parlour chair at Joe's head, no expression on her face. She turned as he came in. He put a hand on her shoulder. He could

feel her trembling. Say something he thought, "What?"
"Your trouble?" Pray! Kneel! He heard himself say:

"Where?"

"What?"

He nodded at the body.

"Nothing, doesn't matter."

"Where was he hit?"

She indicated the covered face and said: "You won't
know him."

He knelt. No prayer came to mind. He knew only that
he was alive and that Joe was dead, and was so ashamed
of thinking this he said quietly:

"I'm sorry, Rachel."

Then George was standing opposite. He lifted the sheet
and Eric saw Joe's face, a mass of congested blood, un-
recognisable. From Joe's dead face he looked up at
George and said:

"Cover him, for Christ's sake cover him."

He felt Rachel leaning against him. George stood and
stared. Eric was trying to hold and lift Rachel and pull
the cover.

"For pity's sake, George."

"For pity's sake, I want to see this proper, and I want
to mind it."

Rachel had fainted. There was a door off the parlour,
a bedroom probably. He got it opened and managed to
get the switch. Striped pink and white paper, a deal floor,
brass bed, a corner wash stand. He placed her on the
bed.

Her face was so cold that he put his hand to her
mouth; breathing all right. Her hands seemed grey. He
took them in his own. When her eyes opened she stared

at the electric bulb, frightened animal eyes that slowly swivelled and then there was such pain and anguish and ravaged incomprehension that it cut more deeply than Joe's awful face in the next room. If there was a living man could speak now, what words would he use. Christ in Heaven what were they, who could speak? Say what? Joe, her father, the awful choking sound of the mother two rooms away, George staring stupidly, what words? And because her face was still and her eyes pouring over, it was worse because she made no sound. If she cried out he could say "Don't Rachel" or "Please" or some word of solace, but there was no word or words, and he knew it and she knew it, and he knew he was crying with her for Joe, for her mother and father, for the whole world. Her lips seemed to move and then she said:

"Loved him, Eric."

"I know."

"Loved . . . he was like . . ."

"Yes."

"Comfort, we're dying . . . love me."

"I know."

"Dying, Eric."

"I know."

And the cry that came from her mouth, he had never heard before, and never wanted to hear again. She made a sort of noise, like something choking. It seemed to come more from her lungs than throat as though she were drowning in grief. He held her.

"I'm breaking inside, Eric, breaking, kiss me, touch me, touch me, love me, comfort me."

As he held her she went limp. He laid her gently

down. Her face seemed whiter than the pillow. She looked dead. Then he heard George shouting. In the silence that followed he went through the parlour. More people in the kitchen now, the R.U.C. District Inspector talking with the Sergeant, Ruth Robinson still stupefied in a chair, the other two women passing round cups of tea. George was staring hard at the superintendent. Then he said with a voice as cold as a chisel:

"One of your rotten breed done this."

The Inspector, a Catholic, did not react.

"Are you deaf?" George shouted, "Yes, you!"

When George said again: "Are you deaf?" the tension altered from grief to a confused hatred. The Inspector turned and said coldly:

"Who's your Commanding Officer?"

No one answered. Then Eric said quietly: "Come on, George."

"Who is your boss?" George asked. "One of them Kennedys and their rotten mafia?"

The Inspector turned and said to his Sergeant: "Get this man's Commanding Officer."

It seemed to Eric that the two women, the Sergeant and the policeman, were all looking at the Inspector with hatred and suspicion. When the Sergeant moved to get Dixon, George said:

"All the one, all murderers."

The Inspector put down his notebook on the sideboard and waited. When Bill Dixon, George's Commandant came in, the Inspector asked quietly:

"Is this man under you?"

"He is, Sir."

"Name?"

"George Hawthorne."

"He has called me a murderer. I have taken note of that, I want you to take note of it and report it."

"I'm not afeered to say what's true."

"Outside, George," Dixon said, ". . . outside."

George left, Eric followed. In the yard Dixon took hold of George's arm and said:

"Talk like that does no good, George."

"You're right, talk's useless, Craig's right. Liquidate them, every last one of them."

"Listen, George."

"Too long we've listened, three years too long."

George wrenched himself away and moved towards the van. Dixon said quietly to Eric:

"Things are bad enough here, take him home, stay with him 'till he cools, that's duty enough for tonight."

Near their van a British soldier was listening to a small pocket transistor. The voice came across the sea, cold and factual: "Word has just come in now that Tom Robinson, father of Joe Robinson the part time U.D.R. man who was shot earlier this evening, has also died."

The voice went on about oil shortages and President Nixon. In the turf shed Eric saw the machine-gunned Vauxhall, army ballistic experts examining it with a powerful torch. He could see blood splattered on the windscreen. More cars had arrived, military, police and private cars, neighbours standing about in groups, not wanting to go in, knowing they must. He saw a British Army officer walking towards the door with a priest. When the priest went into Robinsons, one of the women began to scream something; it sounded like "Fenian Bastards, Murderers!" he was glad George was in the

van and not in the house. He started the engine and
drove slowly through the lighted yard and the uniformed
figures, towards the main road.

"Left, take the low road," George said.

For a moment Eric hesitated; it was two miles longer,
but he was not going to argue. He turned left. For miles
not a word was said. They were stopped twice at army
check-points and quickly cleared. At Latgallon quarries,
George said:

"Pull in here."

"What?"

"I have to stop."

Eric drew in behind a gravel dumper. Mid way in the
cratered quarry of crags, rock face, and jutting limestone
rose the black scaffold of a grading machine, topped by
a hut. Beyond it and below five acres of worked over
quarry and rock pools, the fields sloped upwards towards
Latgallon. George got out and went over behind the
dumper. Eric checked that both rifles were still in the
car. A dog barked somewhere, a military convoy passed.
George was taking his time. When the windscreen got
muggy, Eric got out and saw the figure of a man against
the sky at the far end of the quarry. The figure was
clear of the quarry, and moving in an upland field towards Latgallon. "Oh God no," Eric thought, and then
called "George, George!" He cupped his hands and
shouted louder "George!" The figure went out of sight.
Eric began to run, tripping over the ragged surface. He
fell cutting both hands and a knee. He got up aware of
blood dripping from his left hand. He put his left hand
in his pocket and kept running. There was a rough staircase of stone hacked out of the quarry face. He went

up them two and three at a time. From the quarry top
the fields switchbacked up towards Cassidy's. No sign of
George, should he call again? Some neighbour, drunk, or
courting couple might hear. He was running as in a
dream. Two fields from where he was he could see high
hedges. He crossed a gate into the lane. He could then see
the lights in Cassidy's yard, the reconstructed cottage,
the new barns, byres and silo pit.

As he approached the familiar hum of an Alfa-Laval
milking pump, the smell of fermenting silage. No sign
of George. He kept running 'till he came to a padlocked
gate. He clambered across it. The lane forked two ways,
one to the house in darkness, the other to the lighted
yard. He could see cows tied in cudding in the herring-
bone parlour. At the yard entry between two out-houses,
he saw what looked like two sacks of meal lying sideways on top of each other. As he neared, with a sudden
sick shock, he saw Willie Reilly humped across a bag of
dairy nuts, sprawled as though copulating in an obscene
posture of death, mouth and eyes open, tongue out. In
the yard, he saw George from the back, driving a graip
into what looked like a dung heap; again and again and
again, and again.

"George!"

Under the 200 watt bulb his uncle's face looked back
in knotted fury, his mouth drooping. He flung the graip
towards the middle of the yard. It spun bouncing and
ringing off the concrete, blood on the prongs. Eric saw
that it was a man's body face down in the dungheap.
George walked to meet him. Eric tried to say something,
his voice made no sound.

"Your bastard brother's in the entry, and that's

Cassidy . . . two for two and no shot fired, let them equal that and don't stand there like a gom, the job's done."

Then George was walking out of the yard and down the dark laneway towards the padlocked gate. The body on the dungheap twitched. Eric's heart was pumping so fast he found it difficult to breathe. He moved towards the body. Cassidy's profile allright, bloody lacerations on his neck and back. He turned away retching.

In the kitchen at Oakfield George filled two mugs with Bushmills whiskey. He drank his own, filled it again, and pointed at Eric's.

"Drink up, son."

"I don't drink."

"Time you started."

The yellow liquid in the cracked mug was the colour of the manure effluent on Cassidy's face. Eric put his hands on the table to stop them trembling. His left hand was badly cut and swollen. He was aware that George had hung his coat behind the door and was examining it, groping in pockets. He then looked down at his boots, examined the soles, first one, then the other. Black, dry and shining, a little mud on the toe-caps. The limestone eyes stared straight. He came to the table to fill his mug again.

"What are you afeered of?"

He picked up the bottle of whiskey and held it. "No shake in that hand; my heart's steady as a rock, and my head; I'd do the same tomorrow or next week. They'll all make noises, but our side'll be glad some men had guts to act; blood for blood, this is a celebration son.

They won't know it was me, but vengeance is done, the job's a good one."

Eric stared. He was insane. The country was full of savage talkers on both sides. He had always thought talk was only talk, and that the men of blood were cold, stupid, and silent, hired by men too clever to take risks.

"Say what's in your head."

"They didn't do it, George."

"Cassidy knows who done it, not just by name, he knows them, he could hand you a list from here to Portadown of all their murdering heroes, age, rank, how many jobs they done, *he knows*: that's enough for me."

"Willie; you knew he'd be there?"

"Luck of the draw."

"Could have been anyone?"

"I'm not in the dock, son."

"You are!"

George smashed his mug on the black stove and began quietly, his back to Eric:

"I do solemnly swear support for King William the Third Prince of Orange and all heirs of the Crown so long as they support the Protestant religion and Ascendancy and I do further swear, I was not, I am not, nor ever will be a United Irishman nor took oath of secrecy to that Society and on no account will I admit a Roman Catholic and I am now become an Orangeman without fear of bribery or corruption and I will keep a brother's secrets as my own."

He had turned from the stove. Eric said without looking up: "Unless in cases of treason or murder."

"You goin' to whine, go to that Papish Inspector, fall on your knees, tell him it was your Uncle George! That what you're going to do?"

"I'll not do that, George."

"Then for Christ's sake stop niggling, the job's done; we done it well."

Eric heard the incredulous pitch of his own voice: "Ah Christ, George, quit!"

"What?"

"We! We! I'm not stupid; you tricked me."

"I what?"

"Tricked, tricked."

"Say your say, go on, say it."

"Dirty . . . yes, dirty, you're bad as the worst of them, you done a rotten thing, and you clean your hands on me."

"Did I ask you to folly me, one single word, to witness what was done? You follied, you saw, you're not fit to stomach what you saw let alone do it, so now you whine 'tricked' . . . you don't know your own mind . . . I do."

He was at the bottle again. Eric noticed a slight tremor in the pouring hand.

"They're lucky."

"Who?"

"Joe, Tom, Cassidy and Willie, the dead ones. I'm going."

Eric began moving towards the door.

"Wait son, stay awhile."

"For what?"

"Stay, please."

That long white face pleading. He had never heard

that mouth say "please". Nausea gave way to a moment
of pity:

"For what, George?"

"Don't cry, Eric, Jesus son, don't cry."

George put a hand on his shoulder and made him sit
on a chair.

"Look at me, son, you know me, don't shake your head
like that, speak boy, open your mouth, you sat on my
knee in this kitchen and . . ."

"George, that's nothing got to do with what we
know."

"We marched together, made hay, cut turf together
we . . . I'm George, your mother's brother, your uncle,
your friend, you know me, Eric."

"I thought I did."

"My life, have you thought on that, no woman, no
brother, no close friend ever, wrought on my lone all
my days, for what? I have nothin' but this house and
forge, a few acres and a stretch of bog but *that* is somethin', land that is somethin' and I've somethin' to tell
you."

"I know too much, George, I don't want to hear any
more."

"Listen son, old Tom's dead, Joe's dead, Rachel and
Ruth, think of them, their men gone."

"I don't want to hear, George."

"There had to be a reckoning."

George held the glass of whiskey towards Eric and
said: "Drink, son, you're like a ghost."

"I don't want to drink or talk of Robinsons, or
Cassidys or Catholics or Protestants, or what's goin' to
happen or what's not goin' to happen."

There was a long silence and then George said: "I'll tell you what's in my head, been meanin' to tell you this long while, no odds about me, I'm for the suit of boards and the clay. I've no money much, but there is this place, and the bog at Kilcrin; it's all yours."

Eric looked out the window at the dark fields.

"Land's gone mad everywhere, even round here they'll pay three prices for it . . . all yours, from this night on."

Land, earth, spades, gravediggers, varnished boxes, women stumbling with grief, men crying. The day after tomorrow four burials between the two churches that faced each other across the river. Machines still on the cows at Cassidy's, kicked off by now. Tomorrow some neighbour or the postman would find them in the yard.

"All yours, eight generations of Hawthornes, yours, I mane it."

Eric did not look at the white blurred face as he said: "I don't want it."

"Take care what you say, son."

"I said it with care, George, I don't want it. Put it on the collection plate, I don't want it."

"You don't talk to me like that."

"How should I talk, what's in our heads now? When we wake; when we meet tomorrow; next day; next week? We won't want to meet. I won't want to work this land, any land about here, ever."

"You're a coward, boy."

"Yes."

"You are . . ."

"Yes, all my life, afraid of you, George, afraid to pick between my mother and father, afraid of God, afraid of Catholics, afraid of dark and dreams, afraid to hate or love ... I'm tired of being afraid ... but if you're brave George, then I'm a coward like my father and I'll stay one."

George stood suddenly. "Your father's son, O'Neill treacherous bloody Irish at the back of it, begrudgers, traitors, turn your back when I need you most."

George was whining now, mumbling drunk. Eric said:

"I dunno why I'm in this uniform, who I'm fighting, or what the fight's about, and when it blows by I'll be elsewhere, anywhere, I'll do anything, but I'll not go through another night like this, I'd as lief be dead."

George suddenly shouted: "You're nothin' to me ... nothin', on you go, empty dustbins in Hammersmith, join your brother Sam and his whorey Papish wife, that's your future if you lave here."

Eric felt anger rising: "And yours, George?"

He left him standing in the kitchen and went out to the van. Then he was aware of George stumbling across the yard towards the driver's window. Eric wound it down.

"Hand back your gun, son, and get to hell out of this country, you're nothin' to me now, do you hear me, nothin'."

"We're both dead, George, when you're sober you'll see that."

As he drove down the lane he could see George in the rear mirror standing swaying against the squat black outline of the forge.

His mother had been crying, his father's face like ash. Both seemed very shaken. His mother said:

"Could have been you, son, and your father, whoever

done it, I hope ..." Her voice choked off in a sort of noise. "God help Ruth and Rachel; what are we goin' to do John?"

"Go to Robinsons'," his father said.

His mother said: "Tell me, son."

"Nothin' to tell, Joe's dead and old Tom, it's an awful house, they don't know what they're doing, you'd best go and help whatever way you can."

"Your hands are cut, son, and your knee."

"I fell."

"You've been crying, the boy's terrified, John."

"Not now."

His father said: "We'd best go."

"God help us all."

"George?"

"Home."

"You saw him home?"

"That's where I left him."

Eric knew they were looking at him closely. His mother said: "The boy's shocked."

As he looked in his mother's eyes Eric thought: what if I said, I saw your brother up at Cassidy's, he's murdered Martin Cassidy and Willie Reilly, and if you go out to the haggard and look down you'll see the lights are still on about Latgallon, and they'll be on all night. I never want to see your brother George again, or hear stupid quarrels in this house, or hear the news on telly, or see daylight, and if you go up to Oakfield now you'll find George three quarters drunk and half mad, and maybe he'll tell you the story himself. His mother came very close to him.

"Are you all right, son?"

"I'm all right mother, I'll wash my hand and put a cloth on it."

His father said: "We'll go."

His mother went up to put on her coat. His father stood and stared at the floor.

"The best people you could meet in a year's travel Joe and Tom Robinson, I've thought some bitter thoughts this last hour. A time like this you start to think, maybe George and your mother are . . ."

He paused, as Eric said sharply: "They're not right!"

"I wasn't goin' to say that, son, but it's a low thing a killing like that, unmanly, father and son trapped in a car, like rats burned in a cage. I've thought and thought of every Catholic man I know, I can't see one, not one, would do such a thing, then bit by bit I start to doubt, maybe Dinny McMahon, maybe if he had drink taken, then you begin to doubt them all, hate them all, that's what's happening, men who don't want to hate are pushed to it, that's what I was goin' to say."

When they were gone Eric washed his hand at the kitchen sink, went to his bedroom, took off his uniform, and lay on the bed in his underclothes. An army helicopter moved up from Robinsons', its searchlight scanning the fields between Robinsons' and Cassidy's, probing ditches, hollows, scrub and gap. Could be they'd find Cassidy and Willie before morning. He switched on the transistor waiting for the next bulletin. When it came in ten minutes there was no mention. His mother and father would be back in an hour or less. He couldn't face any more talk about Robinsons. He tried to lie still and close his eyes. They were pulsing under the lids. His body was trembling. With an effort of will he could stop it, but moments later it would start again. From where he lay he could see the winch gibbet on the gable wall of the byre where he had talked today with Maggie ... a hundred years ago. When he closed his eyes he could see Willie Reilly across the bag, his tongue out, George like a clip from an old film, ramming away with a steel fork, the crowded kitchen, Rachel's eyes pouring over. All this was more frightening when he closed his eyes. He kept them open and looked out the window again. Then the board ceiling lit up and he heard the engine of the old Bedford, the squeal of the back springs as it crossed the gulley. Silence. Two doors closing, his mother and father talking in the kitchen, then his mother.

"Eric."

He replied, his voice strange. They were at his door. As the door opened he said: "Don't put on the light."

His father came into the room, his mother stood at the doorway. Even from the low light in the hallway he could see how drawn she was. His father said:

"You go on, Sarah."

To Eric she said: "Good night, son."

His father moved to the window: "The world's a midden, a bloody midden ... birds are lucky and trees."

"You were a brave while."

"We came back by George's."

He knows, Eric thought, and asked quietly: "How was he?"

"On the floor in his own vomit. I put him to bed, your mother cleaned up."

"Did he say much?"

"Raved, something about 'Christ in the fields'."

"What?"

"Christ in the fields . . . raving."

His father moved from the window, sat on the side of Eric's bed and lit a cigarette. "Sam's well away from it all."

"Yes."

"Dead, you're good for nothin' but the ground; I think you should go, son."

"I will."

"When?"

"Tomorrow."

"Where?"

"Across the water, anywhere."

"You might have to stay a brave while."

"No odds, I saw and heard enough today, to keep me away a brave while."

"You're right, try and sleep."

"And you, Da!"

Two hours 'till daylight. He closed his eyes and turned from the window. A helicopter like a gigantic hawk whirled silently over the beech copse, a searchlight moving from tree to tree. Birds in outline perched in stuffed stillness on black branches. The pelts of badger, fox and otter, battened to trunks. Soldiers and masked men moved in shadows outside the copse. The searchlight moved to the centre of the clearing. From a gibbet over a huge stone hung a cage full of men and women, fear and hatred in their faces. Beside the stone the Rev. John Plumm read soundlessly, solemnly from the Bible. Below him Maggie Reilly, sow-like, confessed to the anus of a curate listening to her leering between his legs, his father behind Maggie on all fours about to mount. The helicopter ascended slowly, the beam of the searchlight

widening. Then Cassidy came into the clearing with a Civil
Rights banner carrying a statue of Christ with a bleed-
ing heart, Willie Reilly walking behind him in his blue
knitted cap. George, crouching behind the stone altar
with a long narrow root scobed out as a collection box
flailed at Cassidy, smashing his skull, driving the other
end of the shaft through Willie's heart. A young British
soldier walked into the clearing with a girl. The girl had
a rosary beads around her neck. They lay down. The
soldier began kissing between her legs. She took a Webley
from her handbag and shot him three times in the head.
Paratroopers directed by a tall British officer ran from
skeletal bushes into the clearing. One of them opened the
cage hanging from the gibbet. As the men and women
came out they were machine-gunned, bodies falling
screaming, coughing, spluttering blood. Rachel in nurse's
uniform watched, a hand on her groin, her face blank
and crying. Sam and Maisie followed by small children
approached his mother. His mother's face was white with
hatred. She ripped open Maisie's stomach with a bread
knife, pulled out a bloody child and smashed its head
against the lectern, screaming "Papist murderers . . .
bastards". Then a great noise of birds, animals and
humans, a noise like a gathering storm, and Eric shouting.

And he was sitting up unable to shout, a retching in his
throat, the sky livid behind the black winch gibbet on the
byre gable. For a minute he sat, his heart jumping in his
chest like a caged animal. The house still. Had he shouted
or dreamt he shouted? He looked at his pocket watch,
6.28, two minutes till the news. He closed his mind
against what he knew. A summer dawn like any other,

sitting on the side of the bed trying not to think of Tatnagone, Oakfield, and Latgallon, looking out beyond the byre to the haggard field, cows cudding ignorant under hedges, swallows skimming low over the humps and hollows of the house field, rain today with that red sky, hay-rot for small upland farmers, growth for lowland silage makers. It must break soon. Police, questioning, back-tracking, threads of uniform on barbed wire and thorn bush, fingerprints on graip and gates, tractor loads of evidence. . . .

"George," he said to himself quietly. "Oh Jesus, George . . ."

Lying in a stupor in the cockloft or maybe having his first whiskey to greet the coming day. The voice came low on the transistor: "Miners, Robinsons, a soldier shot dead in Belfast, two bombs in Lurgan, Nixon, nothing." He dressed quickly and went out to the hallway in his bare feet, avoiding boards that creaked, his father deep asleep, a grey faced, open mouthed corpse. His mother's door closed. Would she wake and call? Silence but for the wall clock in the lower hall beside his Grandparents. He stood in the glass porch listening, the tiles cold under his feet, looking at the sloping yard, the out-buildings stepping down. Always this way. It would stay this way for a hundred years or more when he was gone and all forgotten. He felt pity for the two people asleep upstairs in their separate rooms, Rachel sitting at Joe's side with her mother, and along with pity and shame. No fear; there was nothing left to fear.

The van was facing the entry. He let off the handbrake. It rolled across the dry yard, bounced over the gulley with a squeal and down by the orchard. Well past the beech copse he let it slip into gear. The engine jolted to life. There would be military checkpoints every few miles, soldiers watchful and jumpy. This was it, a dull red glow in the east, the small odd-shaped fields, bushes, rushes, his heart pumping steadily. Desertion? The coward's way? Maybe, who'd know: George?

Christ! He came on them so suddenly he almost braked, two Saracens across the road, about a dozen soldiers, one of them waving him down from a hundred yards or more. His right foot hovered over the brake, the soldiers grouped round the big rubber wheels, all moving now. He could see their faces, the waving soldier moving backwards.

Now! He put his foot on the accelerator, saw them move apart, some go behind the Saracen, others falling on their stomachs. A flash came from the left ditch, glass shattering; pain, and the old Bedford skidding sideways before it lurched tumbling across the ditch, his lungs bursting, dying, yes, dying, blood in mouth and eyes, done, yes, over, and then as the Fermanagh uplands dimmed he heard Yorkshire voices far away, one saying:

"Christ knows, he's Irish, mate; they're all fucking mad over here; shoot first, ask after."

Other books from The O'Brien Press

Anthropology / Folklore

PASSING THE TIME
Folklore and History of an Ulster Community.
Henry Glassie. HB

IRISH FOLK HISTORY
Folktales from the North. Henry Glassie. HB

TO SHORTEN THE ROAD
Folktales from Ireland's Travelling People.
George Gmelch & Ben Kroup. PB

TINKERS AND TRAVELLERS
Ireland's Nomads. Sharon Gmelch. HB

Archaeology

VIKING DUBLIN EXPOSED
The Wood Quay Saga. Ed. John Bradley. HB

Architecture / Environment

BUILDINGS OF IRISH TOWNS
Treasures of Everyday Architecture.
Patrick & Maura Shaffrey. HB

STEPS AND STEEPLES
Cork at the turn of the Century.
Colm Lincoln. HB

YOUR GUIDE TO PLANNING
Ed. Patrick Shaffrey. HB & PB

IRELAND'S SHOPFRONTS
Screenprints by Dee Parfitt.
Text by Patrick Shaffrey.

WHERE THEY LIVED IN DUBLIN
John Cowell. HB

URBAN IRELAND
Development of Towns & Villages.
CDU. HB & PB

Art

IRISH ART HERITAGE
from 2000 B.C.
Hilary Gilmore. HB & PB

Biography and Memoirs

VOICES OF IRELAND
Donncha Ó Dúlaing. HB & PB

ME JEWEL AND DARLIN' DUBLIN
Éamonn Mac Thomáis. PB

THE LABOUR AND THE ROYAL
Éamonn Mac Thomáis. HB & PB

GUR CAKE AND COAL BLOCKS
Éamonn Mac Thomáis. HB & PB

JANEY MACK, ME SHIRT IS BLACK
Éamonn Mac Thomáis. PB

YOUR DINNER'S POURED OUT
Paddy Crosbie. PB

Children

FAERY NIGHTS
Oícheanta Sí
Stories on Ancient Irish Festivals.
Mícheál macLiammóir. HB

JIMEEN
An Irish Comic Classic.
Pádraig Ó Siochfhradha. HB

THE LUCKY BAG
Classic Irish Children's Stories.
Ed. Dillon, Donlon, Egan, Fallon. HB

Fiction

HERITAGE and Other Stories
Eugene McCabe. PB

THE OPERATION
Gordon Thomas. HB

ISLAND STORIES
Tales and Legends from the West. CDU. PB

HEROIC TALES
from the Ulster Cycle. CDU. PB

PROUD ISLAND
Peadar O'Donnell. PB

THE LAST SANDCASTLE
Jeremy Leland. HB PB

THE BEGRUDGERS
John Cowell. PB

THE WRITERS
A Sense of Ireland. Ed. Carpenter/Fallon. HB

OUT OF FOCUS
Alf MacLochlainn. HB

THE BEST FROM THE BELL
Great Irish Writing. Ed. Sean McMahon.
HB & PB

Classic Irish Fiction Series

AFTER THE WAKE
Brendan Behan. HB & PB

THE DIVINER
Brian Friel. HB & PB

THE PORT WINE STAIN
Patrick Boyle. HB

THE BIG WINDOWS
Peadar O'Donnell. HB & PB

THE FERRET FANCIER
Anthony C. West. HB

THE WEAVER'S GRAVE
Seumas O'Kelly. HB

Food and Drink

1000 YEARS OF IRISH WHISKEY
Malachy Magee. HB

WILD AND FREE
Cooking from Nature.
Cyril & Kit O Céirín. HB

General / History

IRISH LIFE
Ed. Sharon Gmelch. HB

**VIKING SETTLEMENT
TO MEDIEVAL DUBLIN**
CDU. HB

DUBLIN 1913 - A Divided City
CDU. HB & PB

**ALL GRADUATES & GENTLEMEN
Marsh's Library**
Muriel McCarthy. HB

CROWN AND CASTLE
Edward Brynn. HB PB

THE CELTIC WAY OF LIFE
CDU. PB

THE QUIET REVOLUTION
The Electrification of Rural Ireland.
Michael Shiel. HB

Industrial Relations

**INDUSTRIAL RELATIONS
IN PRACTICE**
Ed. Hugh Pollock. HB PB

**REFORM OF
INDUSTRIAL RELATIONS**
Ed. Hugh Pollock. HB PB

Island Series

SKELLIG
Island Outpost of Europe. Des Lavelle. HB

THE BLASKET ISLANDS
Next Parish America. Joan & Ray Stagles. PB

**INISHMURRAY
Ancient Monastic Island**
Patrick Heraughty. HB

Music

THE VOICE OF THE PEOPLE
Songs and History of Ireland.
Mulcahy/Fitzgibbon. PB

Nature

IRISH NATURE
Norman Hickin. HB

NATURE IN ACTION
Young Readers Ecology Handbook. CDU. HB

Politics / World Affairs

INSIDE THE EEC
An Irish Guide. Barrington/Cooney. HB & PB

WORLD SURVIVAL
The Third World Struggle.
Gráinne O Flynn. HB

SEEDS OF INJUSTICE
Reflections on the Murder frame-up of the
Negros Nine in the Philippines from the Prison
Diary of Niall O'Brien. PB

Practical

GOING SOLO
An Introduction to the World of Work
for the Teenager. CDU. PB

WORKING TOGETHER
The Co-operative Concept
Pat Bolger. PB

Reference

A BOOK OF IRISH QUOTATIONS
Ed. Sean McMahon. HB

PICTORIAL IRELAND
Yearbook and Diary 1986
Full colour. Wiro bound.

PICTORIAL LONDON
Yearbook and Diary 1986
Full Colour. Wiro bound.

Topography / Travel

**Day Visitors Guide to the
GREAT BLASKET ISLAND**
Ray Stagles. PB

FIELD AND SHORE
Daily Life and Traditions,
Aran Islands 1900. CDU. PB

A WORLD OF STONE
The Aran Islands. CDU. HB & PB

**IN WICKLOW, WEST KERRY
AND CONNEMARA**
Gmelch/Saddlemyer. HB

**MEDIEVAL DUBLIN - Two
Historic Walks**
Bride Rosney and Ian Broad. PB

Send for our catalogue of books — and also if interested ask for the list of educational books from O'Brien Educational.

All enquiries to 20 Victoria Road, Dublin 6.